CHARMED

A HAVEN REALM NOVEL

MILA YOUNG

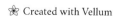 Created with Vellum

Thank you for purchasing a Mila Young novel. **If you want to be notified when Mila Young's next novel is released**, please sign up for her **mailing list** by **clicking here.**

Your email address will never be shared and you can unsubscribe at any time.

Join **Mila Young's Wicked Readers Group** to chat directly with Mila and other readers about her books, enter giveaways, and generally just have loads of fun!

Join the Wicked Reader's Group!

I've had so much fun writing these fairy tale retellings and I hope you enjoy them just as much.

Each story in the Haven Realm series is a standalone novel and can be read in any order, though the more tales you read, the more likely you'll meet familiar characters.

These are adult fairy tale retellings for anyone who loves happily ever afters with steamy romance, sexy alphas, and seductive fun.

Join My Wicked Reader's Group!

Enjoy!

Mila

CHARMED
A Haven Realm Book

Arabian Nights. Three Dangerously Sexy Genies. A Deadly Sorcerer.

Abandoned by her mother at a young age, and left to survive in the slums of the Utaara, Azar must steal for survival. Sure, a life of crime has no honour, but if it feeds her brother, she'll do whatever it takes. Whispers speak of a desert cave where the Sultan stores all his treasure. Stealing some jewels is worth the risk to afford the medicine to cure her brother's illness.

In the depths of the Sultan's cave, she finds a brass lamp and unleashes three gorgeous genies. Except they are weakened from being trapped in the lamp for hundreds of years, and of not much use. Azar's plans turn for the worse when they are captured by the Sultan's evil vizier, who wants the genie's power to feed his dark magic. Can she defeat the vizier, resist the genie's allure, and save her brother before it's too late? Or will they all meet their fate at the hands of the vizier?

HAVEN REALM

The realms of Haven warred for ages upon ages, laying devastation upon its lands and its residents alike. To put an end to the death and destruction, the realm was divided into seven kingdoms, one for each race, ruled by nobility, entrusted to maintain the truce. Over centuries, kingdoms rose and fell as the power of the ruling noble houses waxed and waned. And the peace between the lands persevered. But a corruption is growing, bringing darkness to the realms, and threatening the return of war and suffering to Haven.

PROLOGUE

"*T*hank you for your business," the shop owner said in his ostentatious drawl as he handed over a brown hessian bag to his client.

The client snatched his purchase as if his life depended on it. He lumbered his heavy frame to the left, ready to depart. A waft of spiced perfume mixed with body odor hit me in the face, making my eyes water. Talk about marinating in the stuff.

Apparently, the rich, fat cat couldn't see past his uppity nose and bumped into me, letting out a startled cry. His droopy, red-eyed gaze ran the length of me, and he shuffled backward. With a loud and displeased sniff, he flicked imaginary dirt off his silk kaftan stretched tight over his rotund belly.

I pulled my cotton shirt tighter over my chest. After all these years, I still wasn't used to the way people normally reacted to my stained and torn clothing, my grubby face, and dirty fingernails. What else did they expect when my brother and I had nothing? Bathing water was a luxury for us.

Clutching his bag tight to his chest, the fat cat waddled

past me, giving me a wide berth, as if I had the gray scale disease.

"Rah," I said, lunging at him with my fingers curled like claws.

He whimpered and scrambled out the door, setting off the tinkling bell in his haste to depart the shop.

A chuckle rumbled in my throat. Served him right for making me feel like the scum of Haven because I didn't come from wealth like he did.

All the while the shop owner continued preparing mixtures of herbs. Like most snobs in Utaara, he refused to acknowledge me, as if serving someone like me was below him.

I cleared my throat. "Excuse me, sir."

Herbs brushed against the bag as they slid from the attendant's metal scoop.

Fire shot through my veins. "Excuse me," I said louder and with more insistence.

Still, he ignored me.

I slammed my palms on the glass counter. "I'd like to buy oil of the dragon thistle for my brother, please."

The shop owner sighed and put his scoop aside. His gaze stained me with the same brush of disgust as the rich, fat cat's. "That's a very expensive medicine," he said in a way that suggested I'd never be able to afford it.

Shish kebab. Sounded as if I'd need to steal something to pay for it.

Well, two could play at his game. I kept my cool, as if the cost didn't bother me. "How much?" I asked, voice steady, refusing to show him he intimidated me.

He folded his fingers together and tilted his head. "One thousand markos. Payment upfront."

My heart shuddered. Damn it. That was the same price my friend, a herbalist, had quoted me. *Gods.* That was a year's wage for a middle-class workers in Utaara. I was a thief, not a worker. My regular haul usually included fruits, vegetables, and meat. I certainly didn't have that kind of coinage lying around. Finding that amount of gold coins would require me to steal an item of significant value. Something I didn't like to do, as there was considerable risk attached. The last time I'd stolen a golden candelabra from a rich, fat cat like the one who had left the shop, I was almost mauled by his guard dog. The time before that, I got tangled in wire on the top of the fence, and the cuts festered, and I needed medication to treat my wounds. If I got caught by the palace guards, I'd leave my brother ill, dying, and all alone.

A lump formed in my throat, making it hard to breathe. "What?" I croaked.

"One thousand markos," he repeated, in his oh-so-high-and-mighty voice, talking to me like I was a child.

Sweat pumped from my body and dribbled down my back. I rubbed a hand on my neck to clear some. "That's outrageous. Are you having me on? What's so special about this medicine anyway?"

The shop owner continued with his duties. "The dragon thistle requires a specific form of preparation to extract the oil." He waved a dismissive hand at me. "Come back when you have the markos."

Two weeks earlier, Ali had fallen ill to a chest infection. The Avestan, the local physician, had said if my brother didn't get herbal medicine, his condition would deteriorate and fast. Stuffy, old fool was right. Ali coughed like hell and some nights struggled to breathe. He grew weaker by the day. Rashes were sprouting up all over his skin. Each day, he ate less and less. Pounds were dripping from his already lean frame.

"But my brother has the dark lung." My hands squeezed the edges of the glass cabinet. "I need this medicine."

"Listen, my dear." The owner's tone lightened a little. "I'd love to help you. But I need the coins up front to purchase the oil. If your brother is ill with the dark lung, then he does not have long."

Tendrils of doom weaved around my heart. My brother's life depended on the dragon thistle oil. I had to do whatever it took to get my hands on the gold coins to buy it.

"Thank you," I said as I exited the shop my mind raging with fear.

CHAPTER 1

*D*esperate times called for desperate measures. Nothing was stopping my latest heist. Not even the protests from my younger brother, Ali. Every night since visiting the herbal shop, I had thought long and hard about how to fix our situation. I was willing to do anything for my brother, no matter what the risk. If saving his life called for me to steal a few jewels from the sultan's cave to buy Ali's medicine, then the danger was worth it. The sultan, along with the other fat cats I pinched from, could afford to lose a few valuables here and there. This condition adhered to my one rule: never swipe from someone who couldn't afford to feed their children.

No one in Utaara knew about the sultan's cave. The only reason I'd heard about it was because I'd stolen a map from the head palace guard. The scroll contained locations of all the sultan's assets; his main residence in the palace, investment properties, homes for his family members, and temples.

"It's too dangerous." My brother begged for the tenth time to give up on the idea, grabbing my arm, but he was too weak to hold on. The hollows in his cheeks and dark circles beneath his eyes aged him beyond his eighteen years. "There's got to be another way."

My heart melted at how frail he'd gotten over the past week. Flu had spread like wildfire through the slums, and Ali and I had both caught it. Damn thing knocked me about for several days. Unlike me, Ali had not recovered. Even as a young boy, he was always getting sick. The Avestan, the local doctor, told me Ali's immune system was not as strong as mine was because my mother had run out of milk and had not breastfed him.

"You know this is the only way," I said to Ali, turning away from those soulful brown eyes before I caved and changed my mind.

It was hard enough, breaking the law. Yeah, the risk was there… If I got caught, I'd either end up imprisoned or lose my hands for committing treason against the sultan. A fate I couldn't afford if I wanted to keep my brother alive. But for Ali, I'd find a way to fly into the heavens.

My hands trembled as I dragged on a brown-cotton kaftan and pants that helped me blend in with the landscape…and into the shadows if need be. Around my face, I wrapped a shawl to protect me from the desert sand.

"We're not living like this for the rest of our lives." I gestured to the pitiful shack we called a house in the middle of the slums.

Wooden shutters hung off their hinges, allowing flies to buzz inside. The pantry door had fallen off, and the mice ran rampant. Pretty much all of our recycled furniture was crumbling—from the boxes and plank for a kitchen bench, to the stained, saggy mattress Ali and I shared. And then of course, there was the sofa, which caused me no end of pain when I had to sew the frays in my clothes where the springs had caught on the cotton.

Ali squared his shoulders.

I kissed his forehead. "I won't be long, I promise."

The wooden cart we used for a table wobbled as I put one foot on it to clasp the buckle of my sandals. Stupid piece of junk. No matter what I stuffed beneath the edge to even it out, it remained lopsided. But for something I'd found by the docks, it served its purpose, and it was more than most owned in my neighborhood.

Without money, I couldn't pay for food, water, clothes, or any of the basic necessities. Every few days, we snuck down to the river for a bath. We were fortunate the sultan provided this free accommodation. Run down as it was. Was it any wonder my brother got sick all the time? Living among the old slums of Utaara, surrounded by squalor, the starving, and the impoverished.

Heck! How was I, or anyone in this city, able to afford any medicine? We were blessed if we had food for one meal a day. But...I counted myself lucky to have a roof over my head. Thank the gods.

I collected my dagger from the table and jammed it into the sheath on my belt. Years of experience, learned from doing this job, had taught me never to leave home without it. Nothing was going to get in my way tonight.

"Azar, please." Ali sat up.

His chest quivered from the hacking, wet cough gripping him. His face was grimy, like our shack, and I sat down again to rub his back.

When Ali calmed and took deep inhales, I ruffled his hair. "Want me to make you a hot tea before I head off?"

I squeezed Ali's hands even though he would not meet my gaze. He reminded me of our mother. Dark-brown, curly hair. Long, thin nose. Skin like the fur of a camel. I must have looked like our father who we never met. Green eyes, lined with long, black lashes. Ebony locks, always pulled back in a braid to keep it off my face. Rounded face and cheekbones with plump lips. Our neighbor had once called me pretty, but I suspected it had something to do with them wanting to borrow money for their daily meal.

My heart slumped against my ribcage as I got up to prepare Ali a mug of tea. At eighteen, he should have been selling silks in the marketplace, tending sheep in the fields, or building new mudstone dwellings. Not cooped up, withering away in a shack, his skin turning paler by the day. Every ounce of me wished for a better life for us both. Jobs. Families. A loving home.

Our mother had abandoned us on the doorstep of the local orphanage when I was ten and Ali six. That place was a hellhole. Mustafa, the institution's master, forced all the children to clean the homes of wealthy businessmen, all to line his own pocket. On the fortieth night at the home, my brother and I ran away, never to return.

My brother was all I had left. My reason for waking up every day. Death was not stealing Ali from me. Not today. Not tomorrow. Not ever.

"Here," I said, handing Ali the cup of steaming tea.

He grunted his thanks, took a sip, and put the cup on his makeshift bedside table. "Karim, come here."

Ali lifted the little Capuchin monkey we called our pet off the ratty, old pillow covered in holes.

For someone roused from his slumber, Karim seemed pretty cheerful, bouncing on the bed, twittering away, then settling on Ali's shoulder.

Such a cute little thing. All black, except for the eggshell-colored fur around his chest, arms and face. Hands the size of a baby's. The most expressive brown eyes I'd ever seen on an animal.

"Don't you go helping Azar," said Ali. "Otherwise, no bananas for you."

Karim tucked his head like a scolded apprentice. He moaned and swayed from side to side.

I tilted my head, marveling at the intelligence of the little critter and how he understood everything we said.

Like Ali and I, Karim had been deserted, too, all for refusing to perform parlor tricks for his owner. I'd found the monkey on the streets, a bony mess with matted hair and a serious flea problem. After a decent scrubbing, and a few meals, he'd come good. Memories of the day I brought him home filled my mind and warmed me. Ali had fallen in love and not stopped smiling for weeks. Damn near broke my brother's heart when I told him it was time to release the monkey into the wild some months later. But the day Karim and I caught a boat up river up to the mountains bordering the Terra realm and I let him go, the little squeaker jumped back onto my shoulder and refused to go.

Keeping the smart, little guy was the best decision I'd ever made. Whenever Ali got really sick, playing with Karim was the only thing that made him happy. For that, I was grateful to the little squeaker. Saved my skin, too, on more than one occasion. I owed him my life three times over.

"Come, Karim." I motioned for my partner in crime to join me.

The monkey glanced from me to my brother as if torn between which master to listen to.

"Karim," I said with more firmness.

Finally, the monkey scrambled over to me, scaled up my leg, and made a home for himself on my shoulder. Any excuse for him to get out of our hovel. Karim craved adventure, just like I did. He certainly didn't say no to a banana treat for helping me steal a meal. We only ever stole leftovers that wouldn't sell…and that included lots of juicy, sweet and ripe fruit for the squeaker.

Come on. I did have a heart. The last thing I wanted was to deprive a stallholders' kid of a meal.

While thievery wasn't exactly a profession to be proud of, it gained me a reputation in the slums, and occasionally, a vendor would approach me with a request to steal various items for them. Mostly paintings, heirlooms, and business ideas. But secrets were worth the most and once earned me a hefty price that tided Ali and I over for six months. Those kinds of deals were few and far between though.

I scratched the monkey's tiny head. "Good boy, Karim."

Ali gave us both a pouty glare.

Cute. But that wasn't going to change my mind. I was getting us both out of the slums, with or without my brother's blessing.

From a secret compartment under my mattress, I collected my bag and rope and tossed them over my shoulder.

Before I left, I gave my brother another kiss on the top of his head, yet he still refused to look at me.

But when Karim squeezed Ali's cheeks, he laughed.

Guess I was going to be the big, bad sister again for the next few days. Tough. After tonight, we'd never have to worry about where our food was coming from ever again.

In the doorway, I glanced back at my brother. He buried his head in the tattered comic book…a discarded treasure he collected every week from the bin behind the newspaper merchant's store.

"Drink your tea, Ali. I love you." The rickety, wooden front door clunked shut behind me.

My heart pinched with regret over leaving my brother. But I wouldn't be gone long.

Picking my way through the darkened, dirty alleys of Utaara, I reminded myself that this was all to help Ali get better. Still, the guilt jammed in my chest that I was going against his wishes.

Light on my feet, I didn't make a sound on the soft, sandy ground.

The sultan didn't approve of anyone roaming the city at night. Bedouin—wild gypsy thieves and murderers—scoured the desert at night and attacked pilgrims on the sultan's road. Six months earlier, the Bedouin got bold, launching an attack on Utaara. The sultan implemented curfews at night, and guards patrolled the city, enforcing his rule. That was enough to make anyone nervous, but not me. I loved the stillness the darkness offered. My best plans were hatched atop the rooftops of the city.

Karim leaped onto the walls, climbing along pipes, clothes washing lines, balconies, and more, following my every move.

The shacks of the slums transitioned into the worker-class region of the city. Tall, sandstone apartment blocks, covered in onion-shaped domes, minarets, and decorated archways towered over me. It didn't look like much at night. But during day, the spoils of Utaara were on full display; radiant silks and tents, colored-tile ornaments in geometric patterns, stained-glass windows, palm trees, and other exotic flowers and shrubs. Stallholders burned incense, flower oils, and candles to disguise the slums' aroma of sweat, dirty water, and hard labor.

The scents of spiced meat and flat bread wafting out of a home hit me, and my stomach grumbled with hunger. Even poor Karim gave a moan, as if he were famished, too. We had not eaten since lunchtime. A few leaf rolls were not enough to tide me over for the journey. But that was okay. Once I got tonight's spoils, we'd be dining on kafta, baklava, tabbouleh, chicken schawarma, and all the falafels our hearts could desire! Our lives would turn around for the better.

With my next stop in mind, I picked a yellow flower from a garden and twirled it between my fingers. At the following block, I stopped to pay my respects to the djinn said to haunt the wall. In Utaarian culture, we believed in all sorts of magical spirits. Farads to watch over and protect our children. Khalils to protect the city from sandstorms. Baans for plentiful crop harvests and an abundance of water in our river. But only djinn had the power to grant wishes to those who left offerings to them. Hence, all the bowls filled with fruit, coins, breads, and even smoked meats, lining the pavement at my feet.

Superstitious—yes! But as children, we were taught by our elders to respect and praise the djinn. Offending a djinn, say, by not making an offering to it, might lead one to be subject to its wrath and to become the recipient of terrible, bad luck. Given the nature of my profession, I didn't want to risk pissing off the djinn and ending up in jail. Even if I doubted its existence. Before every mission, I made sure I lit a candle. So far, I'd always had good fortune. That was the way I hoped it stayed.

I dropped the flower into one of the empty bowls. Using a match from a packet someone had left, I lit one of the candles that had gone out.

"Mighty djinn," I said. "Grant me good luck on my mission tonight."

A breeze picked up, which groaned and blew out all the candles.

Strange.

I tried again to light my taper.

Along came the wind again, knocking over the candle, and it rolled along the ground.

I gasped and stepped back. This had never happened before.

For a third time, I attempted to light it, but the match

wouldn't even spark. I went through at least four match-heads. Nothing. Wind buffeted the pack out of my hands. Matches scattered everywhere along the pavement.

My stomach locked tight. Had the djinn just refused my wish? If so, that did not bode well for the task ahead of me. Maybe I should postpone it. But I couldn't. Ali needed the medicine urgently. I had to do this. With or without the blessing of the djinn.

As I strode away, I tried to shake some sense into myself. The candle blowing over was nothing more than the wind. Maybe a sandstorm was coming. As for the matches, well, some jerk had left a dud pack that didn't light. The whole incident didn't mean I'd land more bad luck than I already had. I mean, shit happened all the time. Ali got sick for one. My neighbor lost all her front teeth. Farhad, a merchant in the market, had a daughter who'd just run off with a shepherd in The Darkwoods. Me thinking I was any worse off was just plain silly.

Voices drifted on the sweet, night breeze and silenced the rest of my analysis.

Heart pounding, I pressed my back against the wall.

Karim was picking scraps out of a nearby bin.

"Come here, Karim," I whispered.

At first, he didn't budge, preferring to fling a banana peel onto the ground. But when I stomped my foot, the little squeaker scuttled over to me. He climbed up me, wrapped his body around my neck, and dug his tiny claws into the side of my head. It hurt like hell, but I bore the pain for the sake of silence.

"Pipe down, okay?" This was our signal for silence. It earned me a chipper, which I assumed was his agreement.

I cocked my head, my ears on full alert, my hand itching to pull out my blade.

Careless, heavy footsteps thumped into the intersection

ahead. Firelight flickered, illuminating the courtyard behind which I hid.

"I hate nightshift," moaned a gravelly voice. "I should be in bed with my wife."

Ice stabbed my guts. Sultan guards. If they caught me, my brother was as good as dead, as they would toss me into prison for years for disobeying the curfew.

"This is the best shift of the lot," replied a man with a much more laid-back voice. "Better pay. No one to chase or fight."

That response scored a bunch of grumbles from the other guard.

Typical, lazy, palace patrol.

Judging by the fading of their voices and the dimming firelight, they headed down along the adjacent row of apartments.

The breath I held in rushed out.

"Good boy, Karim." I scratched his chin and earned a squeak of appreciation.

I continued at a hurried pace, entering the wealthier section of the city. Here, the grandiosity of homes scaled upward in proximity to the palace. Polished granite houses with immaculate gardens hidden behind stone walls, decked with swimming pools, cabanas, and Arabian horse stables. All the pleasures money could buy.

Beyond this, four golden domes atop the palace's towers sprouted up like mushrooms in a forest. I wondered what it would be like to live inside those walls, with all the ponds, gardens, servants, finest silks, pillows, rugs, and furniture carved from oak. Never having to worry about where your next meal came from. I pictured myself sitting by the pool eating a bowl of grapes while someone fanned me. Ha! As much as I loved that idea, I wasn't sure I had the stomach for deals, scheming, and arranged marriages. Give me the slums any day over that crap. But I'd certainly take their money.

I climbed a few fences to cut down my travel time and avoid the palace. Too many guards crawling about the place.

Karim showed his displeasure of one particular property by leaving a little gift for the owner outside their garage.

I giggled into my hand. Cheeky little thing.

Based on the position of the moon right above me, about half a rotation of the clock had passed when I reached the desert beyond the walls of Utaara. A barren sea of sand lay before me as far as the eye could see, where few chose to wander, except the Bedouin tribes. Those people did not obey the sultan's rules and had no honor, raiding other tribes and murdering for territory. Savages.

Not that a thief possessed much more dignity. But pretty soon, I wouldn't have to worry about my honor. All my crimes would be forgiven in the gods' eyes when I used my wealth to fund a school and home for orphans.

Sand trickled through my sandals, scraping my feet. Wind tore at my shawl, and wisps of dark hair flicked in my eyes. I rubbed my arms to chase away the chill carried on the desert air. Or was it my nerves stirring the goose bumps on my flesh?

Thank the gods, I had chosen a relatively still night to visit the sultan's cave. The desert of Utaara could be a cruel place during a sandstorm.

Fires blazing in the darkness signaled the Bedouin camps. Best to keep a great distance from them. I kept one hand on my dagger sheath in case of danger.

Among the sand dunes, Karim exploded with chatter on my shoulder after keeping silent for so long. I smiled. His noise was a welcome distraction from the worried thoughts swarming in my mind.

My stomach knotted at the task ahead of me. Stealing a

few jewels from the cave officially topped my list of most-difficult heists. Luckily, I never went into a mission without a plan. Two nights spent scoping out the cavern had revealed ten palace guards posted outside the entrance each night. Instead of patrolling the place like the Sultan paid them to do, they drank wine and played card games, gambling away their wages. Typical. Though I guessed they had to entertain themselves somehow in such a boring job.

If I succeeded in stealing some treasure, Ali would be safe, and we would be set for life. If I failed, I'd secure the standard thief's punishment—severed hands—possibly served up with a gang rape from the guards. Sure. A morbid thought. But when I thought about it, what more could I expect…a young girl, alone in the middle of the desert, with no one to hear me scream. I shook my head. The knot in my stomach tightened at the risk I took for this heist.

Up ahead, the rocky caves rose out of the sandy landscape.

I rubbed my hands even though nerves spiked in my blood. The sultan's treasures and my future awaited. We approached the cave from the west to avoid being seen by the guards. With each step a deep dread settled in my stomach, but I pressed on.

Karim gave me a soft chirp, as if reminding me not to worry because of all the times he'd save my butt before. Smart-ass.

In moments, we'd reached our destination—a hole in the roof of the cave, small enough for me to fit through. From what I could tell, the treasure was stored in an adjoining cavern. This section of the chamber wasn't lit, and I'd be able to sneak in the back way.

By now, my gut ached with worry.

I secured my rope to a large rock.

"Go on, Karim," I whispered.

He climbed down into the darkness.

Just like I'd taught him, he yanked at the rope to tell me he'd reached the bottom.

Time to get a move on. I wound the rope around my thighs to act as a harness. While I lowered myself into the cave, the cord dug into my legs, cutting off my circulation. I bit back the pain. It was a small price to pay for a lifetime's worth of treasure. The instant my feet struck the sandy floor, I unhinged the rope from around me and left it dangling through the hole in the ceiling. Hopefully I'd be able to find it again on my way out thanks to the moonlight trickling through the hole.

Centuries worth of dust filled my nose and made me want to sneeze. But for the sake of my mission, I held it in, even though it scratched and tickled like mad.

Ready for a new future, I whispered to Karim. "Show time."

But as I took a step, my foot got caught in a crevice, and I tripped, twisting my ankle. Staggering pain shot up my leg. Panic pressed to the back of my throat, threatening to escape along with the scream I clamped down on.

Oh, crap! This was the last thing I needed.

CHAPTER 2

*D*espite a twisted ankle, I couldn't stop now. I'd come so far. Letting my brother down was not an option. We needed a life free of stealing. A life free of squalor and grime. A life free of worry and illness. The chance to make a difference and help other kids in need. Those thoughts rocketed me forward with hopped steps.

About one hundred feet ahead, fire burned on sconces mounted to the wall. Golden light spilled out from an opening in the tunnel.

The dread in my stomach turned heavy and thick like quicksand. From my surveillance of the cave, I hadn't been able to determine if guards were posted in the treasure cavern. But I had discovered that every few hours, the guards took turns to replenish the sconce kindling in the treasure chamber and the tunnel.

What if guards happened to be in the chamber doing so when I entered? Then how would I complete my heist? The little voice in my head reminded me that I'd come so far, and I couldn't give up now. Heart still thumping, I snuck up to the edge of the wall. I pulled out a compact mirror from my bag and angled it to see inside the cavern.

My breath hitched. Treasure filled row upon row of shelves. Rubies, sapphires, emeralds encased in rings, necklaces, and earrings all winked at me, urging me to try them on. Candelabras and small statues offered to take their place on my new dining table. Chests containing secret contents begged to be opened. Gods, I had never seen such wealth in my life.

Fire scorched my veins. All this horde could feed the poor and starving people in Utaara. If only I could carry back more to help everyone who needed it.

Something scraped inside the cavern, alerting me.

I scanned with my mirror. Two guards. Brawny and probably lacking in brains. Dressed in standard-issue black pants, red sash, white vest, and turban. One took a leak down the opposite end of the cavern. The other wandered down the furthest row of treasure. Both carried curved swords capable of slicing me in half.

I swallowed the rock in my throat. With my injured ankle, I wasn't fast enough on my feet to get in and out. But I'd be dammed if I'd come all this way, only to hurt myself then hobble back in agony with nothing to show for my painful journey. I didn't have time to wait around all night for them to leave. My brother needed me. Looked as if Karim would have to do the honors tonight.

"Karim," I said, my voice low and urgent. "Get the jewels, boy."

Giving me a little squeak, he scampered off into the cavern, grabbing a necklace with enough rubies to make a queen jealous. He wrapped that and a pearl one over his neck.

Yes! I did a fist pump. Those would fetch a fine price. Good thing I had taught him so well.

He returned, gave me the items, along with a matching pair of earrings and a bracelet.

Gods. Selling these would garner me enough cash to last a lifetime.

I stuffed them inside my bag and fetched a bit of bread I'd been saving for this occasion. "Good boy."

He wolfed down his reward and went back for more treasure.

I kept an eye on him in my mirror. On his next haul, he returned with a cone, fitted with bejeweled rings, and a hair clip set with jewels.

"Good boy," I said, giving him another reward. "One more time, boy."

Karim snatched the bread and went back for round three.

By now, the guard had finished his pee and was heading my way.

The other one admired a sack of coins, glanced around, and then stashed the pouch between the sash and his pants.

What a fool. No thief stole coins. They jingled and drew attention. But I'd keep that intelligence about them stealing while on duty up my sleeve in case I got into trouble. What would the sultan do if he discovered his guard had also stolen from his cave?

Karim was trawling through a treasure chest when one of the guards stumbled down his aisle. Alarmed, the monkey dashed behind a stack of golden plates.

The guard's eyes widened as he spotted Karim. "Bring those back, you little rat!"

My heart beat to each of Karim's furious scampers toward me.

Upon reaching me, he launched up onto my shoulder and dumped his stash into my bag.

Pain blazed through my ankle and foot as I retreated

down the darkened cavern. But I ignored the extreme discomfort. We had to get out of there.

"Where are you, you little wretch?" roared the guard.

Shadows stretched down the tunnel as firelight illuminated it from behind me.

"Hey, get back here, thief!"

Echoes of his shouts battered my ear.

Oh crap. Now we were busted. I almost swallowed my tongue. We couldn't get caught. Not now or ever. Adrenaline pumped through my veins, pushing me harder and faster. Gods, my ankle hurt like nothing I'd ever felt. But we had to keep going.

Karim twittered in my ear and jumped up and down on my shoulder.

"Going as fast as I can," I said.

Boots thudded behind me as the guard gave chase.

My pulse skyrocketed. At this rate, I wasn't going to escape, and the end of my life flashed before my eyes. Ali left alone in the world. No one to fend for him or get him his medicine. The Avestan, carrying away my brother's dead body for cremation. Sobs racked my chest.

Up ahead, something glowed red on the walls. What the heck was that? Some sort of trap? The sultan's weapon? Karim shrieked again and leaped off me, making for the pulsing void in the wall.

"Karim, no!" I hissed against the pain blazing up my leg now.

Ali would kill me if I didn't return with his pet.

That was the least of my worries. Behind me, the tread of the guard grew louder, closer. Each step vibrated through my bones.

I glanced over my shoulder.

The guard was gaining speed, and only fifty feet separated us.

Dread squeezed my lungs. My hands tightly clasped the hilt of my dagger ready to make use of it.

In front of me, Karim hurried back, carrying something metallic, glowing with red letters I didn't understand. What was that? Another treasure? Looked magical with the freaky-red radiance. Whatever it was, it'd fetch me a handsome price and was going in with the rest of my collection. In the Darkwood forest, a woman known as The Collector amassed magical items. Bet she'd pay me a fortune for something like the thing. So, when Karim bounced onto my shoulder, I snatched the item from him. About the length of a banana, it was smooth and rounded and had a spout, reminding me of a teapot or something. Probably inlaid with jewels. A thrill skated down my arms as I dumped it inside my bag.

The guard closed the distance between us.

"Get here, thief."

A rough hand seized my shoulder, sending my pulse orbiting into the heavens. The guard twisted me around to face him. His eyes glimmered with the satisfaction of apprehending a thief.

I was tall and slender, built for sprinting, jumping, and fast getaways. Not for taking on burly soldiers much bigger than I was. Besides, with my twisted ankle, I wasn't exactly in ass-whooping condition. But I gave it a shot, anyway, kicking him where I knew it'd hurt him most. A whoosh of air rushed out his mouth, and he bent over. His face and neck flushed red.

Wiggling from his filthy grasp, I backed away. My ankle was killing me. I'd used it to support myself when I'd launched my attack. Bad move. But necessary to save my life. I didn't get two feet away before he grabbed my wrist. His fingers dug into my flesh so hard.

Now I was one hundred percent convinced the djinn had cursed me with bad luck. Never before had I been caught.

Repeated punches to the guard's head and neck failed to gain me my release.

Karim joined in the fight, slashing at the brute with his claws.

Startled shrieks rang in my ears. The guard seized my monkey and threw him aside.

A scream tore from my lips. "No, Karim!"

The guard grabbed me by the throat. "Give me the treasure, bitch."

Terror wedged deep in my chest. I pulled out my knife, slashing his arm, and he let go of me with a howl.

In return, he slapped me so hard I swear my brains rocked like a ship on stormy seas. The dagger dropped from my grasp and hit the rocky cave floor.

Karim hissed at the guard, and the man laughed, taking a swipe with his foot.

A hard punch knocked me to the ground with a crunch. I landed right on the large, metal object inside my bag. Scorching pain flooded my chest. I gasped for the air that had been knocked out of my lungs. That wasn't the only pain riding inside me. My throat, wrist, ankle, and head all ached. Quicker than a striking viper, I rolled off the object digging into my breasts and scrambled across the rocky ground, out of the guard's grasp. My hands fumbled for my blade, but he kicked the knife aside.

Shish kebab. Now I was in deep camel dung.

Something hissed in my vicinity. Red mist swarmed all around me. The vapor circled me. Terror clogged my throat. *Crap.* What was that? It seemed to be coming from my bag. Some poisonous vapor or something? Released when I fell on top of my bag? Had the sultan set up booby traps in his cave to ensure a thief never got away with his loot?

I don't know why, but all this excited my monkey, and he jumped up and down, clapping.

The guard blinked and wiped his face. Then he licked his lips, as if tasting my death. He yanked my bag off my shoulder.

My stomach sank, along with my hopes of saving Ali. I shuffled across the jagged ground, trying to get back my satchel.

A cruel laugh echoed in the cavern as the guard scuttled out of the way of my grasp.

Coldness spread across my body as the guard emptied the contents of my bag. My breath hitched as I laid eyes on the brass lamp covered in glowing letters. Red steam piped out of its spout.

"That's a genie lamp," he snarled, trying to "Give it to me."

A genie lamp? What planet was he on? My bag contained jewelry and a teapot that was probably loaded with a poisonous bomb that I accidentally set off.

Genie lamps only existed in the bedtime tales my mother used to tell Ali and me before she left us. Surely, if such a treasure existed, I'd have heard whispers of them or would have been asked to steal one. If what the guard said was true, where was the genie? I didn't see any bald, fat-bellied, hairy, old man with a moustache leering over me, ready to blink me back home. A thief like me wasn't lucky enough to find something so rare. Karma had come back to bite me and leave me in deep crap.

"What lamp?" I panted, wrestling the guard. No way was he stealing my loot. Even if it was laced with dust, poison, or whatever. "This is my dinner."

"Sure, it is, *thief.*" The guard reached out with grubby fingers to snatch up the lamp, but the treasure lurched away, as if sucked by an invisible magnet. It disappeared into the blackness...taking with it any hope I had left of ever seeing my brother again.

Karim's screams echoed in the cavern as he raced after the lamp.

A cold shock ran down my spine. Way to go. Abandoning me when I needed him the most.

The guard loomed over me. He sized me up with his cold, pebble-sized eyes, like a lion preparing to kill a gazelle. "What did you do to it, witch?"

He stomped at me, and I scrambled backward, hitting the wall of the cave.

"Nothing." My throat constricted at the notion of being cornered. Every part of me ached, and I wasn't sure how much longer I could continue to try to fight my way out of trouble.

An idea came to mind, one I thought might distract him and allow me time to escape. "If you want it so badly, why don't you go look for it?"

A war of choices waged in the guard's eyes. Duty to apprehend me and take me to the sultan versus claiming the stupid lamp and never having to work another day in his life. In the end, the later apparently won out, and the creep took off.

Yes! I stuffed the jewels back inside my bag and staggered in the direction I had entered. My breaths came hard and fast. It hurt to breathe where my chest had struck the lamp. My flesh there felt tender, telling me a great bruise had formed. A trivial matter compared to the life ahead of me now I had my treasure.

Where the hell was my rope? I scanned the walls, not finding it. Had I taken a wrong turn? Now I might need to climb out.

Gods. What was I going to do about Karim? *He better come back soon.* I couldn't leave there without him. But if waiting around for him meant my death, then I had to make a choice. My brother would hate me for abandoning his pet.

Boots thumping on the rock echoed down the tunnel. Firelight illuminated my path.

"Hamid, where'd you disappear to?" a man called out.

Crap. Someone was coming. The other guard. Armed with a torch.

My bowels turned to water.

"You're not stuffing more coins down your pants, are you?" He laughed.

My gaze landed on an opening in the ceiling thirty feet to my right. I wasn't going to reach my rope in time, so I had to change my plan. Climbing the wall was going to hurt like hell but had to be done. I shuffled across to the opening.

"Hey, what are you doing in here?" the guard shouted.

Damn it. I'd been spotted. Firelight bounced everywhere as he sprinted toward me.

Hooking my fingers into the rook, I hoisted myself up. A whimper flew past my lips. I stuffed back the burn and reached for the next handhold. Fear propelled me higher.

"Your buddy lost his genie lamp," I called out, hoping this one might join in on the search, giving me a free ticket out of here.

No such luck. He reached the wall, dropped his torch, and began his ascent. Of course, he was much faster than I was. Then again, he wasn't sore all over and carrying a rolled ankle.

He grabbed my foot and yanked.

I dug my fingers into the rock for grip. My nails scraped from his repeated tugs. *Shish kebab.* If he did that again, I was going to fall.

"Get down here," he yelled. "In the name of the sultan."

A final jolt tore me loose, and I screamed. My back jarred as I crashed to the ground. Tears stung my eyes, and I rubbed my back. Now I couldn't run if I wanted to. I could barely move without raging pain.

The second guard stripped my bag from me and emptied the contents "My, my...stealing from the sultan. Let's see what his vizier has to say about this."

My stomach hardened like rock as he dragged me along beside him.

The vizier? Gossip on the streets of Utaara told of his cruelty. Torture to extract information. Sabotaging his colleagues to claw his way to the top.

My whole world crashed to the floor and split into thousands of pieces.

Ali. The medicine. Our future.

* * *

SHADOWS SWALLOWED me as two guards from the cave hauled me into the depths of the dungeons beneath the palace. Prisoners moaned. Hands stretched out, as if begging for assistance. But I had nothing to offer them. The place stunk like blood, sweat, piss, and excrement. Water dripped, staining the walls with red.

"No, please, let me go," I pleaded.

Hay on the dusty, stone floor kicked up as the guards dragged me into a grimy cell.

"My brother's sick and needs medicine. Please, don't kill me. Who will care for him?" I asked.

The guards slammed me into the wall. I wheezed from the impact.

One of them put chains on my wrists. I flinched as he clamped the latch.

The two men stepped back and looked me up and down. The guard who had arrested me clutched the hilt of his sword, as if reminding me of my punishment.

My heart pinched. "Please." My shackles clanged as I

yanked at them. I straightened my back, even though the heavy chains weighed me down.

I wasn't below begging when it came to Ali's life. But my appeal to the guards' hearts failed to soften their resolve. With sinister smiles, they left me there. The slam of the heavy, iron door vibrated through my bones.

Darkness crashed in my mind. Here I would remain for the rest of my life. Torturing myself over the death of my brother. Adding more scratches in the wall to mark the number of days of my captivity.

My mind jolted. What about Karim? Where was my monkey? Left to die in the cave? My heart crashed to the bottom of my rib cage. I'd let the monkey and my brother down.

My ankle and back throbbed. I inched up against the wall, stretching my legs out straight. There I sat until I fell asleep.

* * *

GOLDEN RAYS of morning light filtered through the gloomy cell from iron bars in the window.

What was Ali doing now? Was he worried sick because I hadn't returned home? How could I have been so stupid to get caught?

The clunk of the iron latch on the door jolted me from my thoughts. Creaks tore through the cell as the door swung open. In strode a man, dripping in robes of the finest silks, his fingers laced with jeweled rings. He had a steely gaze, stiff jaw, and cold eyes. The savage cut of his moustache ended in a sharp point like a knife. Judging by the snake symbol on his necklace, this was the vizier. My punisher. The taker of my hands—the one tool I needed to keep my brother and me alive.

Coldness spread from my stomach to my toes.

The two guards who had brought me there followed him inside.

The vizier gave an irritated flick of his wrist, as if telling the guards to proceed. "What are the charges?"

The guard emptied the contents of my satchel at his feet. "Stealing from the sultan's cave." His words came out stuttered as if the vizier terrified him.

But his statement caught his superior's attention, and the polishing of his snake-headed staff ended.

He grabbed my chin and squeezed hard. "A crime punishable by death." He twisted my head from side to side. "Pity. An exquisite street rat such as yourself would have made an excellent addition to the sultan's harem."

Disgusting pig. Is that all he regarded me as? A plaything for the sultan?

"Never!" I wrenched my face free.

"Spirited," said the vizier, apparently amused. "I like you. Perhaps I shall keep you for myself."

Every nerve in my body screamed at me to spit in his face.

The guard cleared his throat. "One other thing, Grand Vizier. The thief found the genie lamp you'd asked us to keep an eye out for."

Oh ,here we go...not this topic. The stupid guard had cursed me about losing the lamp for the whole camel ride back to the palace. Well, if there really was a genie, then where was it? Certainly not here, saving my ass. Stupid thing had abandoned me to die.

"You're confusing some other piece of the sultan's treasure for the lamp," snapped the vizier, as if the guard wasted his time.

For the first and probably last time during this unpleasant visit, I felt inclined to agree with the vizier.

The guard gripped his sword hilt tighter. "Smoke came

out of the lamp. When I tried to grab it, something…magical sucked it from my grasp. I searched everywhere. It just disappeared. Unless the thief's rat has it." The last part he growled as he glared at me.

"He's not a rat," I countered. "He's a Capuchin monkey."

"Where is the lamp, street rat?" snarled the vizier.

Whoa! He believed in it, too? Was everyone around there going mad? There was no genie. Just a smoke trick causing red steam to pipe out of the lamp.

I frowned. Okay…say there was a genie, then maybe Karim had claimed ownership of it. That would explain why it hadn't come to my rescue. *Gods.* I hoped he hadn't wasted the wishes on bananas.

My heart splintered at the reminder of the loss of my ticket out of Utaara. My cure for my brother. Our future.

"I lost it," I mumbled to the vizier. "Why do you care anyway?"

Darkness brewed in his eyes. "I've been searching for it for centuries."

Good one, you crazy, old creep.

He raised clenched fists to the sky like a living cliché of an evil sorcerer. "With the genie's power, no one can stop me."

I wanted to laugh in his face. But I held it in. Maybe I could bargain my way out of this. I was a thief. Maybe I could steal another lamp for him.

Before I got my chance to barter, he turned to the guards. "Find it," he barked. "Bring it to me at once."

Both guards stomped out of the cell and down the passage.

The vizier's glare drilled into me. A black flame sprang up on his palm.

My stomach pinched. He had magic? *Gods.* Talk about putting my foot in my mouth. The vizier really *was* an evil sorcerer. That explained his desire to find the genie lamp. He wanted its magic for himself. Images of destruction crashed in my mind. I shoved them aside, not wanting to contemplate that possibility further. This guy was a lunatic.

Smoke poured off his flame and snaked through the air, hitting me. Nausea rocketed through me, and I hunched over, groaning. Every muscle and tendon in my body ached and weakened, and I could hardly hold my back upright. Something about his power caused a violent reaction within me.

Alarm coursed through me. "What are you doing, you creep?"

Malice swept across the vizier's face. "Taking your life force, dear street rat."

Streaks of green traced through the dark flame—the same color as my eyes. The plumes of green turned black as the evil power consumed my life force. Dark clouds poured into the vizier's chest. In my mind's eye, I saw a dark flame burning in the place where his heart should be. I almost shit my pants. He smiled and released a sinister laugh. For a fraction of a second, his skin turned gray, and then it flushed with youth. My youth!

My throat seized, and I gasped, unable to breath.

"With the power of your life force," bragged the vizier, his eyes turning black from the power radiating within him. "I will be able to live another fifty years without aging."

Fear thrashed in my head. Fifty years? Is that all my life was worth? That bastard!

Coldness crawled across my body, as if I were trapped in the snowy mountains of White Peak. It consumed all my warmth, slowing my heartbeat and pulse. All my strength and energy flowed out of me and into the dark flame. The skin on my arms pruned like a date. I felt my cheeks and jaw sag with age. So, this was what death felt like. Panic squeezed my chest. I yanked at my chains, trying to escape.

My feeble actions only made the vizier laugh.

Repeated attempts to break free tore at my wrinkling skin, bruising me.

Unable to get loose, I considered again the sinking reality I'd die here.

Ali.

Karim.

I'd let them both down.

An unexpected heat chased away the iciness consuming me. Ruby-red fire swirled around me in a protective blanket, cutting off the dark smoke nipping at me.

My chest heaved, and I gasped. At last, my breath flowed again. Pity the dark magic had drained me. It felt as if I'd had that nasty flu again ten times over, my lungs stinging, breaths raspy.

A ball of ruby fire exploded out of my mouth, flinging the vizier backward. He hit the wall with a loud crack.

Shock pressed the back of my throat. What had just happened? Some sort of magic had saved me. But how? I didn't possess any.

A vague recollection swept through my mind. That same color red had glowed on the lamp as Karim had carried it to me. The genie! I glanced up, expecting to see some hairy-chested, fat, old man standing at the door, Karim on his shoulder, both waving at me as the chains on my wrists fell off. No such luck.

Then how the heck was I going to get out of here?

That question didn't get an answer. The vizier climbed to his feet. How? The impact of that crash should have injured an old fart like him.

Words tacked to the back of my throat.

Black smoke trailed behind him as he stalked forward.

My insides iced over again.

He grabbed me by the hair and yanked my head back. "You claimed the genie?" A sinister edge clung to his words.

"What?" I was so drained of energy I could barely think straight.

"You rubbed the lamp."

The vizier stamped his long staff, and I flinched.

"I cannot kill you with magic if you are protected by the genie's power," he said.

What was this creep on about? I hadn't rubbed the lamp. I only touched it to jam it into my bag. That hardly counted as rubbing it to release a magical creature from inside.

A menacing gleam captured the vizier's face. "Your genie will be weak after its release from captivity. Presumably hiding somewhere, regaining its strength. But it will turn up soon."

A threatening laugh spilled forth as he rubbed his hands.

"I have the perfect plan to draw it out of hiding," bragged the vizier. "I shall kill you the old-fashioned way. With my pets. Then I can claim your genie and its power for myself."

A vice clamped around my lungs. I'd believe in the genie when I saw it. But for now, I wanted to scratch the vizier's eyes out. That bastard! Wanting to kill me for his own sick pleasure.

CHAPTER 3

"Guards!" shouted the vizier.

In seconds, two more of the sultan's soldiers entered the cell.

"Take her to the pit," growled the vizier.

My stomach locked tight. "No."

Panic kicked in as they removed my shackles.

The slums were wild with stories about the sultan's pit, which consisted of towering walls with a sandy surface in the middle. Gladiators fought to the death there. Rich, fat cats crowded the stands overlooking the pit, betting money on the winners.

Hands as strong as steel clamped down on my arms, cutting off the circulation.

The chasm in my stomach deepened.

"No," I shouted, as I was dragged out of the cell. The vizier's dark flame had drained me of energy, leaving me as limp as a week-old sprig of parsley. I couldn't fight if I wanted to.

Pain flared in my ankle as my feet bumped in grooves in the stone. The guards carried me out of the dungeons, down darkened corridors, and out along columned walkways. Up ahead, a massive, circular structure, like an amphitheater, rose up.

The pit.

Terror slashed at my insides as they tossed me in, and I landed on my hands and knees. I flinched as the doors slammed closed behind me.

The walls were made of some sort of slippery cladding with no indents for grip. Pretty much impossible for me to climb out of there.

The vizier sat up in the stands overlooking the put. No fat cats surrounded him. Guess my death was a private affair, designed for the vizier's eyes only.

Something crashed against the steel roller door to my right. Growls sounded from behind the barrier.

An icy fear clamped around my guts.

Chains rattled to my right as someone opened the roller door.

Adrenaline pumped power back into my body. Muscles taut, I backed away, preparing for the worst.

"To a long and painful death, street rat," said the vizier, menace ripe in his tone.

My heart felt as if it stopped for a moment, as three tigers trotted into the ring.

Shish kebab.

Somehow, I had to survive before my heart exploded from terror.

Two of the felines crept toward me, shoulders and head hunched. Claws slashed the air, and I leaped backward. I landed badly on my twisted ankle, and I winced.

The vizier clapped and laughed.

I would have made a run for the door, but the guards slammed it closed, and I jolted. My head spun with terror. I was dead for sure. Unlike the evil vizier, I wasn't convinced the genie was coming to my rescue, which meant I had to find a weakness in the pit's walls and fast. As a thief, I was the queen of exploiting these kinds of situations. But these walls looked well engineered, smooth and solid and without a single flaw I might take advantage of. Bottom line, no one was getting out of there. To even try such a feat with three tigers stalking me would lead to certain death.

When one cat swiped at me again, I kicked the air, eliciting a snarl from the beast that curdled my blood. The move cost me dearly, pain wise, and my ankle almost gave out. I cried out in pain and terror.

All this entertained the vizier greatly, and he hooted. "There's no escape, little street rat," he shouted.

If I ever got out of there alive, I'd kill that sick creep.

A squeaking sound from the opposite side of the pit caught my attention.

My jaw fell open.

Karim! How the heck did he get here? It would have taken him hours for someone as tiny as him to navigate back from the cave. Oh, I didn't care. My heart was elevated just to see him again.

Gods.

The little squeaker was carrying the genie lamp in his hands. How had he found it? Something inside told me the genie had returned Karim to me, had somehow placed him there with me in the pit. I didn't know how. I blamed it on my strange, magical connection to the lamp—the same one that had saved me from the vizier's magic.

Karim tossed the treasure into the middle of the pit, and it landed next to one of the tigers.

"The lamp!" shrieked the vizier. "Guards, get the girl! Leave the lamp to me."

The door rolled up again.

Well, if the vizier wanted the treasure, then so did I. Hope exploded in my chest. Maybe if I got to it first, I could use it as a bargaining chip. My life in exchange for his precious lamp. If only I could get my hands on it before the tiger shredded me to pieces.

One step forward earned me a savage growl. The cat scratched at the ground, warning me to steer clear of its prize.

"No," I said.

This only angered the tiger further. It snaked forward and batted away the lamp.

Crap.

To add to my worries, a smoky black hand extended into the ring, circling the lamp.

Double crap. The vizier was using his dark magic.

The instant his freaky magic touched the lamp it flared ruby red. An explosion of magic expelled his dark power out of the pit, and the vizier roared with frustration.

I grabbed the sides of my head, trying to still the confusion ricocheting inside my skull. What was that red glow? From where had it come? That same magic had repelled the vizier's attack on my life force.

A fire of determination coiled around my spine. My brother's life rested in my hands, and I couldn't give up now.

Two of the tigers sniffed the lamp. The last trotted closer to the guard, who was enticing it with a piece of meat on a long pole. Face taut with concentration and fear, the guard tossed another juicy treat into a cell, and the tiger followed after it. Once the beast was fully inside the enclosure, the guard slammed the door shut.

One down. Two to go. I prayed to the gods, asking them to bless me. I needed the other two tigers to turn their attention toward the guard with the meat, which would leave me with the lamp and a clear escape route.

In the meantime, something told me to try a different

approach with the beasts. In the animal kingdom, a creature had to command power to dominate others. So I lifted my fisted hands above my head and waved like the angry stall owners did when they chased me after I stole their merchandise.

The tigers growled and backed away, obviously confused.

"Kill her, you fools!" The vizier's tone promised death if the cats failed.

One tiger bounded forward, claws raking the air so close to me I screamed.

My stomach plummeted. "Damn it." A rush of pain seized me as I swept my foot, spraying the nearest cat with sand.

The feline rumbled and shook its head.

"Here, kitty, kitty," said a guard, tossing a lump of meat into the sand.

This captured both cats' interest.

Good. The distraction allowed me to swipe the lamp. Despite my doubts regarding the existence of genies, I rubbed the damn brass with the fury of a soon-to-be-dead woman. Red smoke hissed as it poured from the spout and pooled on the ground and swirled upward.

Apparently, all this action spooked the tigers, and they mewed like giant kittens, warily stalking around the smoky haze. For a few moments, I had completely forgot about them.

A human shape formed in the vapor.

Maybe the vizier wasn't so crazy after all. Had I really just summoned a genie? Gods, I hoped so. I could do with a wish right now. Top of my list—get me the hell out of there. Second and just as important—save my brother.

The smoke molded into strong, muscled legs covered by billowy pants that started at the knees. Well-built arms sprang from a vest barely covering a hard chest. Chiseled jaw, smooth, tanned skin, and brown eyes, like cinnamon with a fiery-red ring around the outside. Hair as dark as the night sky, shaved above his ear, the length pinned back in a long ponytail. A little beard plaited and bound together draped from his chin.

Gods. I shuffled backward, taken aback by his beauty. I felt a tug at my heart.

The genie touched his chest, as if he felt the same thing too. He got down on one knee. "Your wish is my command, Master."

Sunlight reflected off the gold wristbands he wore.

Crap. Right when I needed to utter a few simple words, like, "take me home," my mouth opened and closed, unable to make a peep.

"At last," cried the vizier, clasping his hands. "Ultimate power at my command."

Damn. All the fear, shock, and confusion had made my brain seize; I'd forgotten the evil vizier wanted the genie for himself. The dark flame spasmed in his palm, as if the prospect of more magic excited it. Smog fanned off the vizier and twisted through the air over the pit.

Crap. That can't be good.

But before I could even warn the genie, yellow and blue smoke began piping out of the lamp, too, curling into two more genies, bringing my total to three. Both men were just as handsome as the first, each in different ways. One a brunette and the other with a gorgeous, golden mane. There went my heart again, twanging like a sitar for all three.

Excitement skated up my spine. I was at a loss for words —something that never happened. I couldn't believe my luck. One genie granted three wishes. Did that mean by unleashing three, I earned nine of them?

The yellow-vested genie, the smallest of the three, gave me a wink and flashed a cheeky smile. "At last, a pretty master." The gold ring in his blue eyes—the same color as his clothes—shimmered.

My gorgeous daydream was suddenly brought to a halt by the vizier's grating laugh and clapping.

"Three! Three!" he cheered.

Above us, lines of dark magic crisscrossed over each other, in what looked like the top of a birdcage.

"A trap," said the red-clothed genie.

My pulse cranked up a notch.

To my left, one a guard looped a noose on a long pole around one of the tiger's necks. It roared, thrashed and scratched at the rope, and the guard lost his hold and fell to the ground. The tiger scrambled away, dragging the pole across the pit.

The other stupid guard tossed in more snacks for the cats. But thanks to the arrival of the genies, the poor animals were too on edge to be enticed.

A blast of black magic sliced the edge of the blue genie's arm, and he jumped back.

Crap. Stupid brain. Too many things to focus on at once. Genies. Tigers. Guards. Evil vizier.

I scurried forward to help the injured genie, but the red one yanked me back, pressing me tightly to his body, as if protecting me.

Gods. He smelled like smoke, coals, and burning wood.

More dark projections flew at us. Black goo stained the sand where I'd previously stood. It burned the soil, and a hole opened in the ground.

I shook my head. My fingers found my temples. This had to be a dream. Magic, genies, and evil sorcerers—none of these things were real. Not in my experience anyway. But when an icy dart struck me, and decay crawled along my arm, I knew this was no dream. My chest thumped from my wildly beating heart. We had to get out of there. But my tongue felt like concrete, and I couldn't speak a single coherent word.

Skin along my wrist erupted in a pale blaze of magical fire that melted the darkness on my flesh.

"Protect the master from the dark magic." The red genie's gruff voice, the sheer hulking size of him, and the way the other two followed his order told me he was the leader of the group.

A pale fire sparked to life on the blue genie's fingers. As quickly as it appeared, it snuffed out. He tried again. Nothing. The red genie got off a few fireballs, but they petered out before they hit the vizier. Beside me, the one in yellow seemed more concerned with winking at me, despite the danger surrounding us. How could he remain so carefree and flirt with me at a time like this?

"Brother," barked the one in red. "Focus."

They were brothers? Didn't look like it. Maybe they had different fathers or something.

The one in yellow seemed to regain his senses. A small whirlwind bounced on his forefinger. He winked again, this time as if showing off, and released his magic at the vizier. His shot jerked around like a drunken tornado. Flushing red, he scratched his head and kicked the sand. But his efforts weren't totally wasted. He'd managed to redirect one of the vizier's blows, and it struck one of the guards dead.

Now it was my turn to laugh and clap. Brilliant. Another round like that and there'd be no one to stop us getting out of there.

I glanced up at the vizier. He raised his hands to the sky, his fingers circling as if evoking something. Ominous, dark clouds brewed overhead. Black bolts of lightning flashed between them. Any moment, the heavens were probably going to unleash acidic rain down upon us.

My pulse banged in my head. We had to get out of there.

"Zand," the one in blue said to the red genie. "Our magic is weak from our captivity."

The vizier had mentioned something about this back in the cell.

"We need to sit with the sacred fire, Dahvi," agreed Zand.

What the hell was sacred fire? Where were we going to get such a thing in the sand pit? Damn it. The gods must have really hated me if they gifted me three weak and pretty useless genies.

Just because I needed more camel dung to deal with, all the commotion of the exploding magic, genie smoke, and the dead guard had startled the tigers. One stalked behind the yellow-vested genie.

"Watch out," I cried. But my warning wasn't fast enough.

The cat slashed the yellow genie's leg. He lost his balance and fell to the ground. Blood stained the sand. His face twisted in pain as he clutched his wound.

Gods. Genies were magical beings. They weren't susceptible to wounds. How many more blows did the gods want to deal me?

I clutched my throat. The sight of blood made me lightheaded and dizzy. Memories flooded back of having to stich up Ali's hand after a bully pushed him into a wire fence. Thankfully, that had only happened once.

"Brother," said Dahvi the blue genie, rushing to his downed comrade's side. Dahvi kneeled beside his brother and held him upright. He tore silk from the bottom of his pants and tied it around the wound to stop the bleeding. Not once did he seem bothered by his own wound from the vizier's dart.

Zand the red genie snuck past one of the cats, claimed the guard's sword, and swirled it around, warning the tiger to back off. Both of the large animals snarled.

Thunder sounded from the clouds overhead. A quake

rocked the ground, and I stumbled over. The tigers scampered into the cell area, as if seeking shelter from the impending storm.

Some relief washed over me. One less thing to worry about. But for now, we had to get out of there, stop the genie's wound from bleeding, and save my brother.

The red genie lifted me to my feet, and I leaned on him to steady myself.

"Get us out of here." My voice soared into panic territory.

His heavy brows pinched in confusion. "Where? We have little magic."

Not even the pain of his wound dulled the cheeky grin of the one in yellow. "To her bedroom." His gaze dipped to my chest.

My cheeks burned. Brazen. I'd love to take him to my bedroom. But not right now. I had to really stamp down that idea in order to focus.

"Can't you pool your magic together or something?" I asked Zand. "Otherwise, we have to get past the tigers."

"I've never tried," he replied. "Kaza, are you strong enough?"

"For her," said Kaza a.k.a. Mr. Yellow. "Anything."

All three genies stood together. Red, blue, and yellow bolts of magical fire sparked across them. A multicolored, magical flame sparked on Zand.

Black bolts hit the ground, leaving long, dripping spears.

Shish kebab.

"Karim!" I screamed, racing over to the edge of the wall. "Come."

He leaped into my outstretched arms. Clutching him tight, I spun around. Another black spear landed in front of me, so close I felt the darkness calling to my life force again. Legs shaking, I dashed back into the circle of genies.

Rainbow-streaked smoke circled around us and then

swept us away a split second before a black spear would have harpooned me. Next thing I knew, the colorful fog deposited us in my tiny hovel.

My brother's eyes rounded like a spooked alley mutt's. "Azar, where have you been? I've been worried sick."

Hah! He'd been worried!

Three strides carried me to his side. Karim leaped out of my arms to give my brother a long hug. He peeped away, as if recounting his horrifying ordeal. Cheeky little devil, getting in before me. Ali laid kisses all over the monkey's head. Karim settled in to enjoy a nice stroke along his back.

I threw my arms around them both, determined never to let go. I'd never been so happy to see my brother in my life. Karim gave an indignant squeak as if he didn't appreciate being squished.

"Err, who are they?" My brother interrupted our miraculous reunion.

I turned to the three genies standing behind me.

Even though he clutched his injury, Kaza gave a wave.

More questions spilled out of my brother. "How'd you all get in here? I didn't hear the door. Where'd all that smoke come from?"

My gut pinched. Too many questions. Many answers he would not like. Especially the part about getting caught and the vizier.

I couldn't think past the intoxicating smell filling my nostrils. Smoke clashing with the smell of rain and flowers carried on a breeze.

Zand took sentry position by the window, pulling back the rag I used for a curtain and peering outside. "We mustn't stay here long, Master," he said, returning the curtain back to its original position and then twisting a ruby ring on his middle finger. "The dark sorcerer and his soldiers will come looking for us."

Icy droplets of sweat slithered down my spine. Damn. Guess he had a point. With a sick brother and three magically weak genies I wasn't exactly packing the punch of an army.

"Dark sorcerer?" said Ali.

My brother wasn't going to stop with the questions until I gave him an answer. But right now I had to clear my head. I'd deal with Ali in a moment.

Ten thousand people lived in the slums. That was a lot of houses to check. It would take weeks for the vizier and his men to search for us. Then again, for the right price, someone might snitch. And I bet the vizier was willing to pay handsomely to find me. Unless he used magical means to track us.

All those notions sank through me like tar.

I crossed the room to the red genie. His intoxicating scent of burning coals and wood clouded my mind. "Can the vizier find us with some kind of magical locator spell?"

"No," he said. "The lamp shields us. The vizier cannot kill us while we are bound to it. But he can hurt us. Right now, we're practically mortal."

Anxiety gnawed away at me. This turned things from bad to worse. Perhaps we should skip town and stay with my friend Scarlet in Terra for a week until the genies revitalized. But would that put her in danger, too?

CHAPTER 4

*D*ahvi tried to guide Kaza to the bed, but the yellow genie waved him away. "Look after the master first."

Blue fire crackled between us as Dahvi inspected my bruises and swollen ankle. I leaned forward and pressed my forehead against his. Out of relief. To ensure he was real. Check that the dark flame hadn't killed me, and this wasn't some sort of sick, screw-you last dream from the vizier. Nope. Dahvi's breath tickled my knee. His forehead blazed hot. Hotter than any skin I'd ever touched. I ran my fingers across his thick, braided hair, and the pendant shaped like fire on his necklace. All real. I was still alive. Thank the gods.

"Master?" Dahvi pulled away, his eyes, just like his body, radiated power, sincerity, and kindness.

The aqua line in his earth-brown irises pulsed, and for the briefest moment I got lost in them. The way he said master danced along my spine and twirled around my ribcage. I could get used to being called that.

"Your ankle needs ice," he added.

Gods. He smelled so good. Like fresh rain mixed with

salty water and the bubbling stream in the woods near my friend's apothecary shop.

His intense stare made me blush. I wasn't used to male attention. When I glanced into those sincere eyes, my pulse sped up. My mind wandered to thoughts of touching him. Running my hands over his hard chest, muscled arms, and flat stomach. Of him kissing my neck and caressing my back.

Whoa! I had to shake my mind off that topic to think straight. No way would someone like that fancy me. I glanced down at myself. Dirt-stained fingernails from climbing the rocks. Scruffy, wind-torn hair. Patches sewn onto the clothes. Grimy street rats didn't rate as "beautiful" in this city. All I was used to was being yelled at to return stolen property or having more goods hurled at my retreating back. The yellow genie must have been mocking me when he'd said I was pretty.

I had to call on every ounce of concentration to recall what the blue genie had said to me. *Ice. Oh yeah. Good one.* I didn't have any money for that. Especially after all the treasure I'd stolen remained in the prison cell. That was a luxury I'd have to do without. Besides, my injuries weren't as urgent as Kaza's.

"I'll be fine," I managed to spit out even though my tongue had twisted. "We need to look after your brother. He needs stitches and herbs to prevent an infection."

Kaza seemed to have forgotten about his injury and pointed at Ali. "You're the master's brother, right? Must be. Same perfect bone structure."

Ali's face twisted with disgust as he cuddled a now snoring Karim.

My hands searched my face for this so-called perfection.

"I'm Kaza." The yellow genie hobbled over to shake Ali's hand. "Your sister's genie. That's my older brother Zand by the window. He's the strong one, and he protects and looks after us."

Zand grunted a hello and nodded at Ali. Then he got down on one knee and bowed. He was obviously the obedient soldier of the pack compared to the joker Kaza.

Kaza patted the blue genie on the chest then grabbed him in a headlock and ruffled his hair. "This is Dahvi, my youngest and favorite brother. He's shy and sweet. That's why all the girls *love* him." He pinched Dahvi's cheeks.

I agreed with the girls. The rings around Dahvi's brown irises were the color of pale sapphires. And my god, those eyelashes. I was a sucker for eyelashes. My friend Scarlet, she loved men's forearms, but they weren't my favorite.

Dahvi playfully punched Kaza back. I could tell from their interaction they cared for each other and had a good relationship. Call it motherly instinct, but I sensed some tension between Zand and Kaza. I didn't blame the leader of the group; being locked up with the same two genies for however long in the lamp couldn't have been fun. Not being able to track the stars in the clear, night sky…that'd probably drive me crazy, too.

"What was your last question?" said Kaza, tapping his lip. "Oh, that's right. We arrived here by travelling via the sacred winds."

Ali mouthed the words *sacred winds* as if he thought Kaza was a kook.

To be honest, I still didn't believe the genies were real. But after everything I'd experienced since last night, I could no longer deny any of this.

Chipper as ever, Kaza leaned on a chair for support and kept blabbering. "I'd bend the knee, as I'm supposed to for the master's family, but I just got attacked by a tiger." He flashed his blood-soaked bandage.

My brother's face blanched, and his book fell to his lap.

"Gods," I said. "Shut up, Kaza. You're scaring my brother."

Kaza gave me a cheeky smile. "Mind if I take a seat? My leg's killing me."

"Azar, what's going on?" asked Ali, his voice barely a wheeze. "What dark sorcerer?"

Words pressed to the roof of my mouth as I prepared myself to explain it all. "Ali, you're not going to believe this." My stomach knotted as I snuggled beside Ali, took his frail hands, and recounted the awful story to my brother.

Meanwhile, Dahvi filled a pan with water. Cupboard doors slammed and he created quite a clamor as he opened and closed them, hunting for something. Probably bandages for Kaza.

Zand remained by the window like a guard dog keeping watch.

By the time I finished my story, questions tumbled out of Ali's mouth.

"Where's the lamp? I want to see it. Where's the treasure you stole? If they're really genies, I want proof." By the end, he was short of breath and coughed.

I patted his back to clear the mucous in his chest. His skin was hot and clammy. Worry ate away at me. His fever had worsened.

Kaza accepted my brother's challenge, wincing as he rested on one elbow. A small, pale-yellow flame ignited in his palm, but it puffed out pretty quickly, and he groaned and flopped onto his back.

Ali crossed his arms. "A parlor trick. Any magician could do that."

"Parlor trick?" Flames flickered in Kaza's eyes.

Ali started laughing and wriggling, as if someone tickled him, and the motion tipped Karim off his shoulder. The monkey squeaked with indignation at having his sleep interrupted.

"Still think I am a magician?" asked the yellow-vested genie.

Ali's eyes were round like Karim's. "You really are a genie!"

I smiled at Ali and gave him the *I told you so* eyebrows.

"Azar, could you make a genie wish for a girlfriend for me?" A coughing fit ended his interrogation.

Kaza whacked Ali on the back, clearing away his hack. "Master's brother, unfortunately, it is forbidden for a genie to make someone fall in love, to bring someone back from the dead, or to heal someone."

My heart settled at the bottom of my ribcage. There went my wish to help Ali. Not that the genies were in any position to assist with their weakened magic.

"But I can still assist you, little brother." Kaza winced as he shifted to face Ali. "I'm the master of all things women. Let me teach you."

"It's true," said Dahvi, his voice echoing from inside one of the cupboards. "He has a million lines to woo women."

Woo women? So old fashioned. I kind of liked the way he talked though.

Ali's mouth twisted, and his gaze drifted upward, as if he imagined using some of Kaza's lines.

I tried not to smile. My brother had never even spoke to a girl. Cursed with shyness, he just clammed up and turned red. Not like me. I wasn't really afraid of anyone…except evil sorcerers like the vizier. I just didn't talk to boys because I didn't trust anyone. Three years ago, I had a brief fling with Nabil, the baker's son, but when he cheated on me, I kicked him to the gutter.

Kaza began offering a few sage pick-up lines to my brother.

Zand scraped a chair along the floor and sat on it backward, highlighting the bulging muscles in his forearms. I imagined them wrapping around me, lifting me up, and holding me tight. Gods. I was reverting back into a horny teenager around these three genies.

Calm yourself!

Zand gave me an assertive smile, full of perfect, straight teeth, as if he enjoyed me watching him.

Drawn to him, I crossed the room. "Why does Kaza's wound not heal?"

"Master, we've been trapped in the lamp for so long," he replied in a gruff voice. "It has weakened our inner flame. As did using our power to save us all from the sorcerer. I estimate I will take at least a week in human time to recuperate and rebuild our powers."

It felt like a giant fist had slammed into my chest, and I struggled to breathe. We didn't have a week, would be lucky to have a few days. The vizier would tear the slums apart, searching for me. I trembled as I pressed a shaky hand to my forehead. Now what was I going to do for my brother and the genie?

"What's an inner flame?" my brother asked.

Zand touched his chest where his heart sat in his ribcage, and my gaze lingered there for a moment.

"Our source of power," Zand said.

The fiery ring in his brown eyes blazed as our gazes locked. Again, he smiled in a manner that suggested he found my admiration of his body amusing.

Heat scored my face. Gods. I had to stop being such a pervert.

"At full strength," continued Zand, twisting a ruby ring on his finger. "Kaza could heal in a matter of hours. But in this state, the wound will kill him in a day or two if I do not find ferrets' leaf to cure him."

By the way Zand's jaw tightened, I knew it killed *him* to not be able to zap some medicine into the room. Apparently, family meant as much to him as it did to me. Hearing how dire Kaza's predicament was broke my heart, and I clutched my chest. The news reminded me of my own troubles with my brother. I hated feeling so helpless. With the genies crammed into my shack I felt even more vulnerable.

I squeezed Zand's arm. Zings of electricity shot through my body. Being so close to him was intoxicating. Sexiness, power, and confidence oozed from his every pore. Insecurity swept across me at my appearance—nothing but an unattractive grub in my filthy rags. Something flickered behind his gaze. His eyes held me in a trap, like a cobra hypnotizing me. I had to shake myself out of his spell.

"I won't let that happen," I promised. "We'll get your brother the medicine he needs."

My stomach twisted into knots. To be honest, I didn't know how I'd do such a thing; I didn't have a cent to my name, and I'd lost the sultan's jewels. But I'd find a way.

Dahvi returned with a pitcher containing the last of our water, bandages and cloths stuffed into the crook of one elbow. He took a seat next to his brother. Something told me he was the brains and the mommy in this family of genies.

"Move over, Brother," said Kaza, pushing Dahvi aside. "Let the master tend to my tiger scratch. I wish to be pampered for a change." He leaned back, locking his fingers and tucking them beneath his head.

For the first time in a long time, I laughed. Not just a quick chuckle, but a deep, hooting laugh, which ended with a snort...much to my embarrassment.

Kaza's mouth curled into an amused smile, as if he found my snorting and blazing cheeks endearing. "Very sexy, Master."

I tucked my head, letting my dark hair fall over my face. Having three handsome males around me at once made me dizzy.

Okay. Focus. Time to clean Kaza's wound.

I dipped a cloth into the bucket and wrung out most of the water. My hands trembled as I removed the bandage on Kaza's leg. Thank the gods, the blood had stopped. But the wound had blackened. That couldn't be good. By the looks of it, he might need antibiotics to prevent the injury from festering further.

Worry began to grind into my temples, bringing on a headache. Going back to the local store for herbs wasn't an option. His prices were through the roof. My friend Scarlet had an apothecary shop in Terra that sold healing herbs. I wondered if she'd take an "I owe you genie wish" as payment.

Kaza grabbed my hand and kissed it. "Tell me your name, Master."

I got lost in the golden ring around his blue eyes. That and the smell of flowers, baked goods, and that electrified scent the air always carried before a storm.

The genie tilted his head and offered a wicked smile. "I wish to know the name of the woman whose breast called us out of the lamp."

"What?" I almost dropped the pitched in my lap. Kaza better stop talking about my boobs in front of my brother.

"Gross," said Ali, sticking out his tongue. "Stop hitting on my sister."

Wrinkles lined Kaza's forehead as if he were confused. "Hitting a woman is forbidden in my culture. A female is to be worshipped and adored like the mother goddess." As he said that last line, he gave me a bold wink.

Cute. But a flirt wasn't going to win me over that easy. The least he could do was poof me into a beautiful gown and take me out to dinner…and he was picking up the bill.

Ali rolled his eyes, as if he thought Kaza was being disgusting again. Comic book back in one hand, Ali pretended to read the pages, although he kept peeking over the rim every few seconds, curiously examining the genie.

To my relief, Dahvi kept my brother busy, by chatting to him about the story in the comic book on his bedside table. My heart melted at how Dahvi interacted with Ali. Nothing was more important to me than family.

"I'm Azar," I told Kaza, using light dabs to clean his wound. "This is my brother Ali."

Ali offered a wave to all the genies and returned to his chat with Dahvi.

Kaza cringed as if he bit back pain. Then he flashed his adorable grin that warmed my chest.

"I knew it," Kaza said. "Perfect bone structure must run in your family."

To be honest, all the male attention made me nervous. I cleared my throat and addressed all the genies. "Thank you for saving me, guys."

A shudder consumed Kaza as he kissed my hand again. "My pleasure."

Zand sighed and twirled his ring even harder. "Always stealing the recognition, Brother."

Sparks flew between Zand and Kaza as if bare steel clashed together. The atmosphere in my tiny apartment thickened very quickly with hostility and choked me. Something funny was going on between the two brothers. When Zand kicked the chair away and returned to his original position at the window to brood, I sensed some residual resentment.

I didn't want to pry, but I assumed the tension had something to do with clashing temperaments. Discord was bound to occur when two strong personalities were stuck together in a small space—like the inside of a lamp! Gods knew, I'd go mad if I could never leave my shack. Sure, I loved my brother, but spending every waking minute with him would drive me batty, too.

Dahvi grabbed a set of cards from Ali's side table, shuffled the deck, and dealt Ali a hand. My brother eagerly accepted, as if wanting to avoid further family squabbles.

Feeling a little awkward, myself, I dove into cleaning Kaza's gash. Thanks to the distraction of his dimples, I managed to remove the dried blood without heaving. His piercing gaze drilled into me, as if searching for my deepest and darkest secrets, forcing me to hide behind my hair and look away.

I grabbed some plum wine from another cupboard, and applied that to disinfect his wound. Kaza moaned and bit his lip.

"For someone several hundred years old, you sure do whine a lot...worse than my little brother."

Everyone chuckled at this.

Kaza's shudder and pain-filled grimace corrupted his fleeting smile.

I squeezed his hand.

"He doesn't look so good," said Ali, poking Kaza's sweaty forehead, accidentally flashing his hand of cards.

No, the genie didn't. We had to do something about the fever. Once I'd bandaged him up, I'd brew him some of Ali's special tea to reduce his fever.

Dahvi laughed, snatched Ali's cards back, and reshuffled.

Touched by their connection, my heart went light and fuzzy. Dahvi treated Ali like a younger brother, and I drew strength from the fast bond they'd made.

I placed a fresh bandage on Kaza's leg and tied it. "How did all three of you get trapped in the lamp?"

The genies glanced at each other as if they hadn't expected my question. Tension clouded the room again, and I braced myself for an explosion.

Zand spoke for them. "Kaza refused to stop lusting over the wife of our last master."

Kaza huffed and looked away.

Whoa! This news helped me understand the conflict between the two brothers. Zand had suffered for his brother's mistake.

My heart sagged against my ribs. I related to this. My mother had left me to raise myself and my brother. These days, I allowed few people into my life because I couldn't trust they wouldn't hurt me. After what my mom had done to us, I vowed that no one would ever hurt me again.

"For inviting her affections and taking her to his bed," continued Zand. "He caused her husband to seek out a sorcerer to curse us all, and trap us in the lamp. There we remained for hundreds of years. His curse stipulated that we would only be allowed out when a master appeared—one who would grant us freedom from servitude." His voice trailed off on the last part.

An ache took residence in my chest. I couldn't imagine the pain of being trapped in a lamp for so long. Missing my brother and only friend. Deprived of my freedom. Denied the opportunity to live life as I chose. Never to see the stars at night. Never to breathe the roasting air of Utaara. Never to hear the sitars playing in the market stalls.

Once I had my wishes, I intended to grant the genies their freedom. Did that mean I was the master prophesied in the previous master's curse?

Kaza's face turned dark, like a brewing storm. "How many apologies will be enough, Brother?"

Zand's burning eyes locked on Kaza. "Master, may I leave your hovel to scout this new city for medicine?"

My breath caught in my throat. "What if the vizier or sultan's guards catch you?"

"I can take care of myself," he replied, tossing one of Ali's robes over his head and vest.

I didn't doubt that. It would probably take four normal men to subdue the large, muscular genie. What if he got injured, too? Or worse? The vizier had magic capable of bleeding Zand's magic. My brain felt ready to explode from all the pressure. After what had happened to me recently, I wasn't sure I wanted anyone else taking any more risks and getting themselves hurt.

"Master." Zand grabbed both of my hands and whispered in my ears. "Beware your heart with my brother."

Whatever did he mean? I wasn't giving my heart to anyone. Least of all the playboy Kaza. I didn't have time for love. Even if I did, I wasn't about to share myself with a genie —or three—who wouldn't stick around once I used up my wishes.

Still, my chest warmed at the concern radiating from the red genie.

"Thank you," I said, touching his arm, my fingers itching to crawl up his biceps and shoulders.

Zand nodded.

My fingers burned to touch him again as he pulled away.

The door banged shut after him.

I set the iron pot on the stove and snapped some twigs for kindling to light the damn thing.

Despite Zand's moodiness, I had to admire his determination to save his brother, even after all they had endured.

Dahvi touched my arm, and I nearly dropped the teapot. "Do not worry, Master. My brother will be back when the master of the lamp calls."

Yeah, well, right now, I wanted to stuff that broody jerk back inside the damn lamp.

I didn't get time to dwell on my annoyance further because Kaza crashed back into my brother's pancake of a pillow as if he could no longer hold himself upright. His skin had paled at least by half. Dark circles bloomed under his eyes. Sweat trickled down his temples.

I rushed to his side and pressed the back of my hand to his forehead. His skin was roasting, and I hissed, jerking away. The infection was getting worse and fast. *Crap, crap, crap. Zand better come back with the medicine soon.*

"Brother," Dahvi said to Kaza. "You must go back into the lamp."

"No," shouted Kaza, startling everyone because he'd been so quiet for so long. "I'm not going back inside that prison."

I took his hand and rubbed it. This always worked to soothe my brother when he felt ill. I swept away a blond lock from his forehead. I couldn't imagine what being cooped up in a lamp for a hundred years might feel like. My soul ached for adventure and freedom just like his did.

"How will being back inside the lamp help?" My gaze jumped between the two remaining genies in my home.

"It slows down time," explained Dahvi. "Easing the wound's progression until we can get the medicine Kaza needs to heal."

I wondered if my brother could go into the lamp to slow down his illness until the genies were stronger.

When Kaza touched my wrist, tingles ran down my spine. "I'll go in on one condition. If the master comes in with me."

Oh, boy. There came that cheeky smile of Kaza's again. The one that made me melt, the one full of dimples that lit up his dazzling golden eyes.

Blood rushed to my cheeks, and admiration filled me that he trusted me to care for him. "How long in my time would we spend in the lamp? I don't want to leave my brother—or yours—at the mercy of the vizier if he busts in here while we're gone."

Kaza's fever-induced-trembling hand stroked mine. "Until I fall asleep."

Ali usually fell asleep in ten minutes. I could manage that. Hopefully, Zand would return with some ferret's leaf tea shortly after that.

The notion of spending alone time with Kaza did something to my insides. Except I was going there to help him… not gawk at him. Still, he was so ridiculously handsome I could barely look him in the eye. My gaze ran down the curves of his broad shoulders, down his strong arms and powerful back. He must have caught me admiring him because he laughed.

Heat claimed my cheeks.

Gods. Where was my head lately? I didn't have time for a boyfriend…let alone three god-like ones. Getting close to them was not an option. Trust did not come easily to me. Not after what my mother had done to Ali and me. My brother was my priority, not feeding the lusty beast inside me. For now, I had to find a way to heal Kaza, recoup the genies' power, and heal my brother.

CHAPTER 5

"*P*lease, join me inside the lamp, Master." His playful tone had turned into a beg.

An animalistic part of me groaned, urging me to go with him. I was curious to visit the lamp and the world of a genie. Was it cramped? Full of silk pillows? A smoky haven? But the sensible, suspicious side of me wanted more answers, to ensure mine and Ali's lives weren't in any more danger than we were already in.

I pulled my hand away and shyly looked away. "What if this is a trick to trap me inside so you three can have your freedom?"

Kaza pointed to Dahvi. "She's smart and feisty. I like her more than any other master we've ever had."

Wow. I wasn't sure how to take his comment. Was it a compliment? Or sweet talk to butter me up and trick me? Either way, my "suspicion radar" was on full alert.

Dahvi sighed behind me as if he were giving up. "If a master commands the lamp, she rules our inner flame, and we may not hurt her." Sincerity rang loud and clear in his voice.

In my line of work, I had to be in tune with my instincts. My gut was well accustomed to warning me of trouble. Of the three genies, I trusted him the most because he gave me the impression he would never lie to his master. That I was safe with him and he would die to protect me.

Kaza gestured with his finger. "Show her, Brother."

Like a striking viper, Dahvi snagged the knife from the kitchen bench.

"Hey, what are you doing with that?" Heart racing, I stood between the genie and Ali.

Dahvi lunged at me with the sharp tip.

I froze and screamed.

The knife connected with a bright-blue force. Light exploded outward, thrusting him into the wall. The blade dropped from his grasp and bounced onto the floor. Where he crashed left an imprint of his body in the bricks.

"Whoa!" cried Ali, scrambling to help Dahvi to his feet.

I rocked back on my heels as the force field evaporated.

Dahvi groaned and rubbed his head.

"Told you," Kaza said matter-of-factly from beside me.

How quickly he had moved left me shaken. So much so I kept dropping the knife when I picked it up from the floor. At last, I got a firm grip and returned it to the cupboard. "Don't ever do that to me again, understand?"

Dahvi gave me a weak smile and rubbed his neck. "Just trying to prove a point. We can't harm you."

While this was somewhat reassuring, it didn't stop the palpitations stemming from the knowledge that the vizier could still kill me using other means.

Kaza hissed and clutched his leg.

Crap. I had to get him back into the lamp to slow the deterioration of his wound. "Dahvi, please protect Ali while I will escort Kaza." I kissed my brother's head. "I'll be back as soon as I can."

Despite the seriousness of the situation, Kaza's eyes twinkled,

promising me trouble...just not the kind I was used to. The yellow-vested genie vanished in a golden haze, leaving me wondering how the hell I was going to go in after him.

"Azar," said Ali, his lips pressed into a cautious line. "Are you sure about this?"

No, I wasn't. A part of me didn't want to go inside the lamp because I was scared of what I'd find. What if I had trouble coming back? After all, I wasn't a genie. What if I was trapped in it? The rest of me begged to explore the once-in-a-lifetime experience.

At that moment, I felt like an excited child had taken control of me. It battled with the wary, older me for dominance. This was so unlike me. I didn't trust others so easily, but something about these genies left me unable to control myself and excited to visit a whole new world.

"If they try anything funny," I whispered to my brother, running a hand across his head. "Take control of the lamp, and get me out."

Concern burrowed behind his eyes, but he nodded.

I stood in the center of my hovel. "Okay. I'm ready to go now."

Dahvi took both of my hands and stroked the back of my wrist with his thumb. His breath quickened at our connection, as did my heartbeat.

I pulled away. My mind sprayed icy water on the warmth pooling below. What were these three doing to me? It was like a spell had settled on me. Was it genie magic?

Dahvi cleared his throat. "Ready to go into the lamp, Master? It doesn't hurt. Promise." He caressed the skin across my wrist with his thumb. "Feels like this."

The fun part of me, the one I hadn't released in years,

wanted to giggle and delight in the chills running up my arm. But I bit my lip, held it in, and nodded.

Static electricity burst all over me. Pale-blue smoke swirled around me, filling my nostrils with the sweetest scent of dates and wine. I felt a tug at my core and was sucked away. Next thing I knew, I stood on top of a slab of marble decorated with a satin recliner, pillows, lamps, and that had what looked like a rectangular pool in the middle. The space wasn't very wide. Maybe thirty feet square. I crossed to the edge, curious about what lay beyond it.

I gasped and jumped back.

The marble hovered atop a whirlwind extending from a bunch of clouds.

Gods. My throat squeezed with terror that I might fall off, and I stepped away from the verge.

Not exactly the luxurious palace I had imagined the genies had spent their last few hundred years.

"Master!" Kaza leaped up from his lounging position on a satin recliner. Being on his feet obviously caused him pain, as he winced and moaned.

"Sit and rest." I wrapped my arm around his waist and helped him lie back down.

"I'm glad you came." His gorgeous, golden-eyed gaze trailed across my face, setting my body alight.

Gods. Maybe coming in here with just him hadn't been such a great idea. I felt as if I was losing control. That wasn't me. The feeling was frightening, overwhelming, and exhilarating at the same time.

I guided him down into the pillows. "Rest."

Please, let him go to sleep as soon as possible. Being so close to him was making me nervous and giving me hot flashes.

"I'll rest with you." He inched up, grabbed me with his

strong arms, and pulled me beside him. The action brushed one half of his yellow vest aside.

Waves of golden, static electricity crackled between us, and he smiled. I had to use all my self-control not to reach over and touch his chest to see if it was as rock hard as it looked.

I nudged him with my shoulder. "You snuggle next to all your old masters, too?"

"Of course." He nudged me back, smirking. "Especially the smelly ones."

We both laughed. His honey tones drove me crazy. I couldn't remember the last time I chuckled out loud. It felt freeing to let loose and relax for a change. Being around Kaza made me forget my troubles and responsibilities for a brief moment. He brought out a sense of fun in me that I had buried long ago. For that, I owed him the world.

"This...I don't know what to call this place." I pointed to the slab of marble we were on. "How is it floating?"

"Magic," he said with a waggle of his brows.

I crossed my arms and huffed. "But you're weak. Was bringing me in here all a ruse?"

Kaza offered me a goblet of wine. I wasn't taking his damn drink until he explained himself.

"Relax, Master," he said as if it was nothing. "It's something I created long ago. To remind me of home."

I scoffed. "You lived on a floating city?"

"Yeah."

He gave me that wicked grin of his, and I felt like I drifted into the clouds.

"You should see Zand's room. All volcanoes and fire. He likes it hot." The last line earned me a wink as he sipped from his goblet.

The way Kaza said "hot" had sounded incredibly sexy.

"What do you do for a living, Master?"

Kaza rubbed the end of my ragged kaftan between his fingers, and I blushed.

"You don't smell like a fishmonger." He grabbed my hand and inspected it. "Your fingernails are too dirty to be a seamstress."

He was toying with me, I could tell, but I let him keep guessing.

"Far too beautiful for a princess," he rambled.

I coughed.

"No. I'm serious. Most royalty I've met would make you want to bring up your lunch." He whispered in my ear. "Inbred."

That had me clutching my stomach and laughing.

He winced a little as he folded his arms behind his head. Obviously, the lamp did not steal away all his pain.

"I bet your talents lie in strategy, quick thinking, and keen observation," he continued.

Now he was really playing.

I began stroking his hair to shut him up. "Shh. Go to sleep."

He moaned and closed his eyes. "You're a thief," he said as if struggling to get the words out. "That's how you found our lamp."

I tucked my head, my cheeks blazing hot as a bonfire. How could he read me so well? Was I that much of a give-away? Right then, I wasn't sure how I felt about him knowing my profession. Did he judge me for stealing from others? I'd never let what someone else thought of what I did to survive bother me before, but now, for some reason, I cared about this genie's opinion.

His fingers interlocked with mine and squeezed. "You must be a hell of a thief because you stole my heart from across the room."

I laughed and punched him in the chest. "Do you say that to all the girls?"

He rubbed a lock of my hair. "Only the sweaty ones who have lots of moles."

Gods. That made me snort. I hadn't expected to have such an enjoyable time with him.

"That's very sexy, Master," he said.

I shoved him in the chest for joking with me. "What makes you think I'm a thief?" I asked, curious how he had me pegged.

He gave me that dazzling smile that took my breath away. "Call it genie magic. When your breast grazed our lamp, we all knew it."

Gods. Not the breast thing again. I swear he said that to get a rise out of me. It was my whole chest, not just my boobs. I had the bruises to prove it!

My gaze dipped to my filthy, ratty clothes and picked at them. Curiosity chewed away at me like a rat. I wanted to know what else the lamp had told him.

But first I had to explain myself. "I steal to feed my brother. I'm not proud of it. We don't have a trade or an education. My brother is sick often and I can't hold down a job if I have to look after him."

Not once did he blink, look away, or even make a face to indicate his disapproval. Who would have thought the joker had a serious side to him?

"Twelve years ago, Ali and I left the orphanage because they abused us," I continued, unable to end my blabbering. "The master used us as slave labor, rather than putting us through school like the sultan demanded of every orphanage."

Kaza brushed away my dangling hair. My whole body buzzed. I didn't want him to stop talking or touching me.

"The thief title is nothing to be ashamed about, my beautiful master."

Despite his confident words, I didn't agree with him. In Utaara, I was a filthy street rat, nothing more. But I had much more to give Haven.

Wow. What a mood killer. I hadn't expected to share my life story. Half of this I'd never even told my close friend Scarlet. But I felt so at ease in the genie's company. As if we'd know each other forever. Talking about all this stirred up my deep-rooted grief and anger. Any second now, those emotions threatened to burst from me like a flooding dam.

I cleared my throat and asked a question to divert the conversation away from me. "How'd you become a genie?"

He examined me for a few moments as if he expected my story to continue. Then he rolled onto his side. "That's easy. A sorcerer summoned me and bound me to a lamp. That's why I have these golden wristbands. They hold me captive to the lamp."

My heart twisted at the darkness to his words. I didn't blame him for being resentful. I'd be pissed, too, if someone had stripped me of my freedom.

"Are you human?" I said, using the question as an excuse to pan my gaze along his fine body. "Where do genies get their magic from?"

For the briefest instant, I caught a red flash of anger in his golden eyes, and he bristled. "I come from a tribe known as djinn."

Kaza's sudden shift in mood, from playful to serious, took me aback. Had I touched a nerve? Maybe I should have just stuck to the jokes.

"Under djinn law, those who serve a human are condemned as traitors to our kind and are banished from our realm." His voice took on a hard edge.

My chest tightened with remorse for him. He was forced

into slavery and didn't agree to it. Could never return home even if I freed him. Never see his family again. *Gods.* I couldn't begin to imagine the pain of it.

"That's not fair," I said, sliding my arm beneath him and snuggled closer, hoping to take away some of his anguish and restore his cheer.

"Careful, Master," he said, turning back to me, slipping his arms around my waist. "You might get used to this."

Yes. Yes, I could. I didn't want to leave the warmth he radiated. From the promise of fun. Having him so close had my heartbeat skyrocketing.

Before I knew what was happening, his lips were on mine, hungry and passionate. I turned toward him, pressing my body closer, unable to help myself. Not that I wanted to stop when I'd been thinking about kissing him since the first moment I saw him.

He moaned, and I broke away.

"Did I hurt you?" I asked.

"You could never hurt me." Kaza's hands glided down my lower back.

I trembled, aching to have him closer. Kaza made me feel irresponsible, fun, and carefree. I hadn't realized how lonely I'd been until today. Too focused on my brother and not myself. Having him beside me stripped my loneliness away. I needed this moment more than my next breath. Maybe a small reprieve from the stresses of life wouldn't be such a bad thing.

He leaned in to kiss me again, his tongue pressing against my lips and parting them. I groaned and grabbed his arm. He held on to my hips and pulled me toward him, never breaking our kiss.

My hands ran down his hard and chiseled stomach.

Firm hands squeezed my ass, and I mewed. He nibbled at

my neck, placing soft kisses there. Fire raged between my thighs.

He glanced up at me with a wicked grin as he tugged the end of my kaftan up.

I snapped a hand across my chest. "Hey."

Kaza smirked. "Don't be shy around me," he said, and I let him slide it off.

I shook, unable to find my words, and my insides burned.

Carefully he slid down the strap of my bra, exposing a breast. His touch left a string of goose bumps in its wake.

"I have a surprise for you." He lifted me into his arms and carried me across the pool.

"What are you doing?" I dug my nails into him. "I don't know how to swim."

The last thing I wanted was for him to throw me in thinking it was fun. The thought of drowning terrified me.

"It's okay, my desert queen," he said using a soothing voice. "I won't do that. I'm just going to bathe you."

Oh. I felt a bit silly and tucked my head. I hadn't been bathed by a guy before. The idea excited me. I hadn't had a wash in a week. Smelling like a fat old man's armpit was not a turn on. I didn't want anything getting in the way of having more fun with Kaza.

The genie winced as he set me down gently.

"You shouldn't have carried me with you sore leg," I said, getting lost in his gorgeous sunny eyes.

"Anything for you." He brushed away my hair covering my chest to examine my body. I did the same to him.

Water in the pool reached my knees. It was a brilliant aqua and glimmered as if the sun shone down on it. I doubt I could drown in liquid that shallow.

"Dip in the water," he instructed. "Then rest on that step there."

That was easy. I did that in the river to wash myself.

Holding my breath, I lowered myself to my shins. The water went up to my lower ribs. I gasped as its cold touch.

"That's it," said Kaza, lifting me up and walking me to the seat.

Kneeling on the step below me, he cupped water into his hands and let it dribble across my naked chest. I trembled with anticipation as his he rubbed the liquid across my breasts and shoulders. Over and over he did this, wiping me clean, wearing a wicked grin, as if he imagined what he was going to do to me. I didn't mind at all, and repaid the favor, brushing water across his hard stomach and his chest.

When he was finished, he squeezed my breast. "The perfect size for my mouth." He leaned closer and clasped his mouth over it, sucking deep, his tongue flicking my pebbled nipple.

I drifted on a cloud, euphoria trickling through me, diving fast to my libido. I fisted his hair. "That feels incredible."

He licked my nipples, tickling them.

I broke into a half laugh, half moan.

"Sexy." He devoured my other breast, his hands grasping my ass, kneading my cheeks.

My breaths quickened from his touch. Blood rushed to the fiery apex between my clenched knees. Every inch of me ached for him.

He released a nipple and glanced at me, arousal in his gaze. His hand sailed down my waist, across my stomach, and parted my legs. His thumb passed over my mound and found my inner lips, silky and ready.

He stared at me as he slid two fingers along my folds. "So wet."

Shyness gripped me, and I was torn between wanting to look away and beg him for more. I swallowed the boulder in my throat, unable to find my words as I rocked back and forth over his fingers. Everything happened too fast. I couldn't think straight and drowned in the excitement owning me.

"You're so beautiful. I want nothing more than to worship you, Master." His devilish smirk had me wetter.

A small cry fell from my throat as my body responded to him. He inserted two fingers into my sex, and I gripped his shoulders, falling apart under his spell as he pumped into me.

I screamed, my body convulsing as Kaza kept his fingers locked within me. He silenced my moans by kissing me. I needed him like I needed air. Right now, I'd let him charm all of me.

"You liked that?" he asked, pulling out of me.

"Damn…yeah." I labored to breathe and quivered from his touch. Muscles in my pelvis contracted as warmth spilled through me.

Our mouths met again, and he lifted me with ease, my legs snaking around his hips. Golden rings blazed in his eyes as he carried me back to his sofa, laid me on it and spread me wide. He lowered himself over me. Wildfire from his skin grazed mine. The tip of his hardness pressed into my entrance, and I moaned. His excitement pushed into me, stretching me, widening me, hurting in all the best ways.

I pulled him tight against me with my legs. His fingers intertwined with mine, and he pressed my hands against the cushions. Each of his plunges brought on a fresh wave of pleasure. A groan rumbled in his throat.

I writhed beneath him, unable to get enough air. But the need to draw a deep breath became less important when he plunged into me, the sensation pushing me closer to the edge of another orgasm. His hands were on my breasts, kneading them, and I moaned.

"Kaza… Oh, gods!"

Without warning, he rolled us until he lay on his back, me

on top of him. I met his strokes, the full force of his desire against my pelvic wall. One of his hands found the curve of my back, and I arched from his touch. My movements brought out an even brighter flame in his eyes.

He gripped my hips, pushing his cock deeper into me. Our breaths merged, short and sharp. Every inch of me contracted, and my lower body shook. I was almost losing my mind at how I felt as if I floated in the heavens.

Our moans grew louder and faster as our bodies clashed in rhythm. Another orgasm rolled through me, fast and strong, washing over me like waves. I screamed, trembling against him, and then collapsed onto him as he kept going, holding me tight. He released a loud moan and stiffened as he came. We lay there, entwined, panting, Kaza stroking my hair.

Strange as it sounded, my world felt perfect...as if this was how being with a guy should always be.

An image of a golden flame flashed in my mind. The color of Kaza's magic. I sensed his heart start, his desire surge, and the pain in his leg swell from what we'd just finished. He'd done something to me. Branded me with his magic.

"What did you do to me?" I said, panting.

"Our hearts are bound now," he said, tracing the shape of a heart on my chest with a perfect finger.

"What does that mean?" I asked, my lungs heaving.

"I've let you into my heart." He squeezed me. "You now feel what I feel, and vice versa."

But part of me didn't believe him. He was the joker after all. How could I let him into my heart when we only had a short time together? Once all my wishes were granted, I'd be alone again. For now, I just wanted to stay content, snuggling into his hard chest, listening to his heartbeat.

He pressed his lips to my neck, laying soft kisses along my

ear. His heart whispered to me that he desired me again, called for me to curl in his arms and fall asleep afterward.

But I knew I couldn't. I had to return to my brother. Get the genies well enough to create my wishes and heal Ali. I kissed Kaza on the cheek and got up.

"Where are you going?" He grabbed my arm.

I pulled away as much as I hated the idea. Part of me toyed with the notion of staying here for eternity and doing nothing more than lying with Kaza, but that was me living in a fantasy land. "I've got to get back to my brother."

Disappointment stormed across his face. "Don't leave. Stay."

Our bond told me he didn't approve of me leaving him. All the women he'd shared his bed with had fawned over him like puppies. He liked to be in charge. The one who'd leave the girls hanging, waiting for him. But I wasn't a little puppy.

Truth be told, I didn't want to go. Inside, I fought a battle between my heart and my head. I just wanted to let my hair down. Stay a little longer. Have that wine Kaza offered me. Play a few games. Laugh and joke with him. Definitely continue where we left off and have another round of mind-blowing sex. My heart pumped with such joy. I think I had a crush on him. That was confirmed when I glanced over at Kaza lying on the couch naked, winking at me, and I almost melted and jumped back in his arms.

But I'd promised my brother I wouldn't be long. Zand might have returned with Kaza's medicine. I needed the genies to save my brother. The responsibility weighed heavily on me. Eventually, my head won out over my heart.

"How do I get out of here?" I said, wading into the pool for a quick dip to wash the sweat and mess from me.

"Think it," he said, "and it is."

Okay... but I wasn't exactly a magical being.

Once I'd put my kaftan back on, my gaze lingered on him

for a few moments. His eyes called to me to stay. *Ugh*. It took every ounce of restraint to drag my lovesick, giddy ass out of there. I wondered if everything that had just happened replayed in his mind like it did in mine.

No. Cut it out. You've got to get back.

Fine.

I kissed Kaza on the forehead. "I'll be back to check on you when I can."

He grabbed my wrist. "Is that a promise?"

"To deliver your medicine personally."

That brought back his delicious smile.

I thought about returning to my hovel and my brother. Smoke furled around me as if responding to my request. The last thing I saw before I was drawn out of the lamp was Kaza blowing me a kiss.

CHAPTER 6

*E*verybody's eyes landed on me when I returned from
the lamp.

Karim jumped up and down on one of the boxes. I gave
him a quick scratch on the chin and he piped down.

"What's it like inside?" Ali asked, spooning a mouthful of
what smelled like spiced lamb stew. Karim jumped onto his
shoulder to sniff my brother's meal. Ali fed him little bits of
vegetable.

Where had that meat come from? We certainly didn't
have the money for expensive treats like that. I wondered if
some collective genie magic had been responsible for our
good fortune.

More amazingly, color had returned to Ali's skin. For
once, he was free of sweat. Was he getting better? My question was answered with a big, fat *no* when a coughing fit
racked his frail body.

Dahvi was seated beside Ali, and patted my brother on
the back until his fit ended.

My heart fluttered with appreciation for Dahvi, who'd
obviously been taking care of my brother while I was gone.

Guilt pinched at me for leaving Ali. Talk about selfish. I shouldn't have put my own interests first or lost myself in a lustful episode with Kaza. Did the other genies know what we'd done? I studied Dahvi, who offered me a smile. Zand stood at the kitchen sink, doing what I think were the dishes. His eyebrows arched as he examined the scrubbing brush and bar of soap as if he didn't have a clue what to do with them.

I held in a laugh, wanting to see what happened next.

The soap slipped out of hands and splashed into the water. As he searched for it, he stirred up a sink full of bubbles.

This had me in stiches.

He swished around in the sink to find a plate. But when he grasped one, the slippery sucker slithered got away and dropped back into the water. If only he had his magic, this might have worked out a little better.

I couldn't hold in my mirth any longer and burst out laughing so hard I snorted.

"What?" He flashed a smile, showing a bit of parsley stuck in his teeth.

That got everybody going. Even Karim clapped and hooted.

Gods. I hadn't felt this lighthearted inside in years. It felt wonderful to have such laughter in my home. For so long, the atmosphere had been too somber.

"Brother," said Dahvi, pointing at Zand. "You have some mess in your teeth."

Zand checked in the window's reflection. "Light my lamp!" His tongue bulged in his mouth as he swiped it across his teeth, cleaning them.

By the time I calmed down, my stomach growled a demand for food.

I leaned over the stove to inhale the cinnamon and

nutmeg odor of the delicious, Fesenjan stew. "Where'd this come from?"

"I got the meat from the market," replied Zand.

Gods. My muscles clenched, giving me pains in the gut. "You didn't use magic, did you?"

His heavy brows pressed down. "No."

Thanks the gods. Then I didn't care how he got it; I just needed something to eat.

It was nice to see his dark mood had blown over.

Zand slapped his brother on the back. "Dahvi needed something to pass the time in the lamp, so took up cooking as a hobby."

I guessed having everything at their fingertips would get a little boring after a while.

"How'd you eat inside the lamp if your magic was weakened?" I asked.

"We're like bears," said Zand, pretending to growl as he handed me a bowl. "We have a hibernation mode."

"Thank you," I told him. This lighter side to him was nice to see.

Pale-red flames flickered for a moment when our fingers skimmed as I accepted the bowl. Tiny fireworks went off inside me.

Dazed by our connection, I bumped into a chair, spilling stew broth onto my kaftan.

The corner of Zand's mouth lifted in a smile as if he knew the effect he had on me. His gaze trailed my neck. "My brother imprinted on you?"

"What?" I touched my collarbone. My skin burned red hot.

Damn. My sex rash. Hope he didn't know what it was. Shame burned across my cheeks. Gods. Zand must think me a slut for sleeping with his brother so soon. To cover my blotchy skin, I put down my stew and yanked my green cotton shawl off the coat hanger on my front door. Quickly, I wrapped it around my neck, face, and head, concealing the evidence of my special moments with Kaza.

All the pleasant memories from my explosive activity with him drained out my toes. I pulled my shirt tighter across my waist, feeling cheapened by what had happened between us. *Gods.* These genies were doing something to me. Bringing out strange feelings. Turning me into a lustful beast and I couldn't control myself.

How was Zand going to react if I said yes? Especially considering they'd all come to be trapped in the lamp first place because Kaza had slept with the former master's wife. My stomach clenched, and I braced myself for an explosion.

"Now you are connected." Zand touched his chest where his heart was, then gave me a kiss on the cheek, as if welcoming me to the family.

What? Was this the same broody guy I'd met earlier?

My breath caught in my throat as he squeezed past me. I was a good foot shorter than he was, and my eye level only reached his chest. The bowl I held out to the side almost dropped as my lustful beast took hold, urging me to run my hands along his rock-hard stomach. It took all my restraint to stuff her deep inside me.

Gods. What were these genies doing to me? I didn't sleep with a guy...correction, a hot genie...this easily. Developing teenage crushes on more than one person—or genie—at the same time wasn't like me. Suddenly, I was convinced the genies had some sort of magical spell over me. In that case, I had to stay level headed until my wishes were delivered. Focus on what really mattered; I had to save Ali and Kaza.

My stomach grumbled, and I sat down, taking a few spoonsful of stew.

Dahvi kneeled on the floor and lifted my foot onto his leg. "The swelling has gone down."

Dahvi's fingers worked their magic as he massaged my good foot, and a groan slipped past my lips. *Gods.* If I had of known what I was missing out on, I would have gotten another boyfriend sooner. Praise to the gods for blessing me with the genies. They were really going to extremes to impress me.

I RAN my fingers along the yellowing bruises on my ankle. Last time I'd rolled my foot, I'd been out of action for two weeks. If it wasn't for my neighbor sharing her scraps, Ali and I would have starved. Time was not a luxury when the vizier and the palace guards were hunting us.

Suddenly, the stew tasted like sand, and I didn't feel hungry anymore. I pushed the bowl aside and turned to Zand. "Any luck with the medicine?"

The red-vested genie scowled. "The Avestan did not have what I needed." His voice was hard and strained.

"But, Brother," said Dahvi, pausing his massaging. "We must get the herbs before the vizier finds us, or Kaza will perish."

None of the genies were dying on my watch. I owed them a debt for saving my life. Honor might not be my middle name, but I always repaid my debts. Anyway, I couldn't deny the selfish voice rising in my head, reminding me I needed these three genies to save my brother. Now that the vizier was out for my blood, I was also dead.

I glanced at my brother, and he pursed his lips.

Zand cleared his throat. "He told me a lady called Scarlet, out in Terra, might have what we're after."

"I know Scarlet very well," I said. "She owns an apothecary store out in the Terran province. She also happens to be my close friend."

Zand's heavy brows relaxed as if this news gave him comfort.

Over the years, she'd helped me so many times when Ali was sick. Couldn't thank her enough. She tried to get Ali's medicine but was unable to without payment upfront.

Terra, where Scarlet lived, was a dangerous province in Haven. Ruled by a strict priestess and her order. Magic was forbidden in Terra, and no one was permitted to enter or leave. Combine that with the guards crawling all over my city, and...well, my skills were really going to come in handy. But I wasn't going alone. Not with my banged-up ankle. One of the genies was coming along with me. Since Dahvi had done such a wonderful job with my massage, he'd just earned himself a ticket. While he might be better at caring for my brother, I believed Zand would do a better job to protect Ali.

Dahvi jumped to his feet. "We must leave at once."

"No," said Zand. "We need to sit and meditate for a few hours."

Whoa. One at a time please.

"What?" I said. Time was of the essence here.

"We need to rejuvenate our power," said Zand. "We'll leave tomorrow."

"Someone has to stay and protect my brother," I said, grabbing another bag with my belongings.

"But I want to see Scarlet, too," said Ali.

"No way, mister." I ruffled his hair and gave him a kiss.

Zand's broody brows pressed lower. "I'll stay. But first we must meditate."

"All right." I sat down beside my brother as the genies sat cross legged on the floor.

"Call our names if there is any danger," instructed Zand.

* * *

THE NEXT MORNING, Dahvi fumbled to grab the lamp out of enthusiasm for our journey to Terra. Cute. Reminded me of Ali in a way. But those sexy and sincere blue eyes set the genie a world apart from that of my brother and promised me a lot more heartache.

Karim squawked at me as if demanding a cuddle before I left. I gave into his request and placed kisses all over his furry little head. Then I set him back down.

In my bag I stuffed some exotic spices, which I would give to Scarlet as she couldn't get them in Terra, and loved the stuff.

"Bye," I said, glancing at my brother, who was still pissed with me and wouldn't meet my eye. My gaze drifted to Zand as I closed the door behind Dahvi and I.

Outside my apartment, warm, midday air enveloped me, caressing my cheeks and promising me the world. It helped clear my head a little and stripped away the strong emotions tugging at my heart.

Dahvi was by my side. "Master, how far is Terra? Will we make it there by sunset?"

I just wanted to lick those full lips of his.

Gods! There I went again. Hormones raging and everything. I had to stop this. Using every ounce of restraint, I buried my attraction…no, my *lust*…for the genies down deep.

Dahvi caught me around the waist. "Master watch…"

But it was too late. I smacked into a rug drying on a line between two rows of shacks. That'd teach me for not watching where I was going.

"Inconsiderate…" I almost said a nasty curse as I rubbed my forehead.

Dahvi gave my temples a nice knead. Then he moved to my neck. My body thrummed from his touch and begged for more.

No. No. No. No. I had to pull away before I allowed my desire to carry me away.

"Zand and Kaza," I said, sidestepping the rug. "Do they get along?"

"For the most part," replied Dahvi.

I noticed his gait matched mine and somehow didn't leave a footprint down the sandy lane we traipsed. Damn, that trait would come in handy on heists.

The whole foot thing reminded me of my ankle. It complained a little with a light ache. But the pain wasn't bad enough to keep me from getting to my friend's apothecary.

We took the corner and headed down another back lane, crowded with wooden crates and empty wine barrels. Laughter drifted from the tavern inside the building. The air carried the scent of baked flatbread and dips from the market several hundred feet to the north. For once my stomach was full and didn't groan at the tantalizing odors.

Okay. I couldn't help but pry. "Why do they seem cross with each other?"

"Kaza has a frivolous past with women." Dahvi's liquid gestures entranced me, and I couldn't take my eyes off him.

Oh no. I was in for trouble then. I'd better not fall for him. My last boyfriend cheated on me. I didn't need any more heartache. But something deep inside me ached for Kaza... for all the genies...and it wasn't just lust.

"It's Zand's nature to be very protective. He doesn't want to see you get hurt." The blue genie's warm blue eyes soaked me up, as if I were a sunset.

Man, I could stare at those babies all day.

Stop! Stop it girl. Get a hold of yourself. Geez. What was that? Like ten seconds? I wasn't doing very well with forgetting about my whole genie-lust issue.

Zand cared about me? Sure, I totally understood the protective thing, going crazy on anyone if they hurt Ali, like a lion with her cubs. A man who would fight to protect me was sexy as hell. I'll be damned if this news didn't make him even more attractive to me.

Dahvi smiled as if he knew the effect his words had on me. "My brother is very passionate. It's the Ifrit fire burning in his veins."

"Ifrit?" I said, tilting my head.

"It is a type of djinn," said Dahvi. "Their power stems from fire. It expresses itself as passion, love, loyalty, and sensuality."

That sure explained a lot about Zand. "And Kaza, what is he?"

"He is a Shaitan," said Dahvi. "His magic wields the power of air, and they are the embodiment of lighthearted, mischievous, carefree and fun."

Yep. That wrapped up Kaza in a nutshell. Nothing, not even a wound from a tiger, dented his stride.

Most of all I was intrigued about Dahvi. Like me, he had a sensitive and compassionate side to him. "What type of djinn are you?"

"I am a Marid," said Dahvi, lifting me over a short iron fence. "Our element is water. We represent emotion, wisdom, patience and intuition."

Ahhh. Totally suited Dahvi.

Something about having them with me made me feel protected and safe. That was a strange thing for me. I'd always been the one to protect and look after Ali. No one watched out for me. This whole genie thing would take some getting used to.

Filled with this new knowledge, we turned another corner of our journey. My foot struck something, accidentally knocking it over. Candles and bowls flew to the ground, spilling coins, fruit, and candy onto the sand.

Gods.

We were at the wall haunted by the djinn.

I froze. Last night, it hadn't blessed my wish for a good mission. Two guesses as to why I'd been caught by the guard. Had I upset the djinn? Knocking over its offerings just now was bound to piss it off even more. What would it do to me in return? Make my eyeballs explode out of my head?

Dahvi ran his hand along the cracked wall decorated in a floral motif. "A djinn dwells here. It is trapped by magic."

I didn't want to hear anymore. My feet carried me out of there. No more curses or bad luck for me. I'd had enough for one day.

But as I turned the corner into the marketplace, instinct flared in my belly, a sign I always had when trouble was afoot.

Dahvi bumped into the back of me. "Master?"

"Shhh." Prickles spread higher into my upper intestines as I scanned the immediate area.

Nothing appeared out of the ordinary. Patrons dawdling along the aisles carrying baskets. Merchants cooking meals on hotplates. The baker stacking more bread on his pile. The butcher wrapping up meat in paper and handing it to a customer.

Most of the traders here barely scraped by, so I stole from the wealthier markets across town. Plus, it never paid to pinch so close to home. People knew where I lived. Taking from these people would be stupid and asking for trouble. In the slums, the merchants in this market always looked out for me, giving me whatever they could spare. But that was only occasionally.

Someone grabbed me by the arm.

My heart exploded, and I let out a nervous squeal.

"Azar, it's just me," said Farhad, the merchant selling fez hats.

I placed a hand on my chest to calm my raging heartbeat. "Farhad, you scared me half to death."

Dahvi stepped protectively between us.

Farhad squinted at the genie, assessing Dahvi. The merchant released his hold on me. "What trouble are you in, Azar? The sultan's guards have been asking around about you."

A new wave of panic stretched through me. Crap! That'd make getting around tough. I trusted Farhad and a few other merchants with my life. But for a few gold markos, what was to stop one of the others from selling me out?

"Got into a bit of trouble with the vizier," I replied.

"Gods! That is a man not to be messed with." Farhad pressed his hands together in prayer and raised them to the sky. "May the gods protect you."

I swallowed hard. Yeah, I was going to need all the prayers I could get.

"Master." Dahvi tugged at my shirt.

I looked in the direction he pointed. Two guards leaned against the tobacco merchant's stall one hundred feet to the north. One smoked a cigarette. The other took big gulps from a hookah pipe. A third wandered between the spice and pastry stands. The hilt of his sword gleamed in the afternoon sun.

I nearly choked when I recognized him as the guard who had arrested me.

"Bye, Farhad." I backtracked, taking Dahvi with me.

A stallholder did a double take as I passed.

"Guards!" the female merchant cried. "There she is. The girl you're looking for."

I glanced over my shoulder. The three guards were on the move, chasing after us. Horror fluttered inside me.

"Thief, stop!" one yelled.

CHAPTER 7

*M*y heart dropped to my toes.

Dahvi grabbed my hand, and we ran down the center of the market, away from the vizier's guards. A kid carrying a tray of meat got in our way. I skipped left, accidentally bumping into a woman reorganizing her stall. She stumbled and her basketful of dates crashed to the ground.

"Sorry," I shouted.

Sand crunched under our feet. It still hurt to put pressure on my ankle, but I couldn't get caught as I had the other night in the Sultan's cave. We needed to hide and fast.

Unable to keep up with Dahvi, I slowed my pace to a limp. My nerves were stretched. I glanced over my shoulder as two guards shoved people out of the way, cutting a straight line for us.

Shish kebab.

I overturned a stall of pastries and a rack of clothing. Merchants shouted curses at me. I heard the guards grind to a halt. The table scraped against the ground, and they were back on our trail.

Dahvi stopped to yank the cloth off a tent and let it fall on the guards. They shouted and scratched to get free.

Up ahead, a man played a flute, charming three cobras in a basket.

As we passed him, the genie kicked the receptacle over, and snakes spilled all over the ground. They reared up, flaring and hissing. Everybody screamed as the place descended into chaos.

Sorry. But we needed something to slow down the guards.

If only the genie had his powers, we'd be out of the mess in a puff of smoke, and no one would get hurt.

"Which way?" said Dahvi as we arrived at an intersection at the end of the market.

I chanced a look over my shoulder. The guard who had apprehended me in the cave jump over the snakes and continue his pursuit.

Crap.

My pulse thundered in my veins. "This way."

We ducked down the next lane to our right.

The genie and I took another right and then a left into the back alleys. I scanned the buildings surrounding us for a way out of this mess. Clothes air-dried on wire stretching between the buildings. Potted plants lined windowsills, their leaves stretching out toward the sunlight. A metal grille crawled up the wall of one of the buildings.

Perfect.

"Quick, up there." I climbed the grille, scaling the sand-stone wall, passing one level of the two-story apartments in a matter of seconds.

"Hey!" shouted the guard as he entered the alley. "Get back here."

Nothing was stopping me from getting to the top.

"Hurry, Master," Dahvi said.

"Can't move any faster with my ankle," I said.

The genie's hand cupped my bottom and pushed me up, giving me the boost I needed.

"Gods!" I said, surprised yet aroused by the position of his hand.

Once I reached the top, I flung my leg over the edge and pulled myself up.

"Here." I offered Dahvi a hand to help him.

Dahvi took my hand, climbed up, and I lead him across four mica rooftops toward the west. Sure, they were dilapidated and old, but I'd been up here plenty of times to star gaze and knew they'd take my weight.

"The guard is not far behind us," he puffed, out of breath from the climb.

My breaths came fast and heavy. Not because of the activity; I was used to sprinting and climbing things. But the adrenaline spiking in my blood was sending my system into overdrive.

"There's a plank over there, where we can cross to the next building." I pointed to the north. "Once we're over, we'll take down the board so he's trapped."

From up there, we could see out across the city. Palm trees along the river swayed in the breeze. Water spurted from the fountain in the city's heart. Golden domes and tiled mosaics, geometric patterns dotting the landscape. The wild desert beyond gleamed a rich orange.

"Spectacular view," commented Dahvi as he lifted me over a parapet. "Reminds me of home."

"Yes," I replied, fighting the giddiness from his touch…or was it the pain in my ankle? I wasn't sure which. "One we don't have time to enjoy right now."

I heard the grunts of the guard from fifty feet behind us. I assumed he was trying to climb the grille. A fat, old, lazy lump like him might take a while to get to the top.

Dahvi stormed across another roof, dragging me with

him as my limp worsened by the moment. Thank the gods, most of the apartment buildings were joined or very close together, otherwise, there'd be nowhere to run. That said, in about another twenty or so rooftops, we'd have to cross the plank to the next block of apartments. From there, we'd have to return to street level, cross the sultan's road, then it was a clear path along the river leading to Terra.

By the time we'd reached the eleventh roof, I glanced over my shoulder.

"Gods," I spat. "The guard's here."

Crap. Crap. Crap. He was faster than I had anticipated for an old guy. Fear thumped in my chest so hard I thought my heart might burst through my ribcage.

The pain in my ankle scaled up three notches as I pushed into a run. I wanted to stop to rest for a few moments but couldn't. Tightness settled across my ribcage as I contemplated the agony of climbing down the next building.

"Master, your ankle," said Dahvi. "Let me carry you."

"No, I'll be okay." I waved him away.

I glanced over my shoulder again, and my breath hiccupped.

The guard was catching up and fast. His eyes blazed with hatred and the promise of death—retribution for all the torture he'd probably received from the vizier as a result of my escape.

Something caught my foot, and I tripped, rolling along the mica, scraping my legs and hands. Pain flared on my grazed knees. A whimper flew out my mouth at the sight of my blood.

"Are you all right?" Dahvi scooped me into his arms as if I weighed nothing.

Something about being curled in his grasp felt familiar. Protected. Safe. But how could I enjoy it with the guard gaining on us?

Terror coursed in my veins as he drew his sword. Metal grating against the scabbard turned my blood to ice.

"Shish kebab," I whispered under my breath.

Dahvi skidded to a halt as he reached the end of the last roof. "The plank's not here."

"What?" My words came out strangled and hoarse.

When he set me back on my feet, I missed his touch at once. I inched closer to the edge, hardly able to bare the weight or the pain in my ankle. One peek over the side revealed what used to be the plank, now nothing but broken shards of wood on the cobbled ground below. *Crap.* Now we were left with no other option but to climb down the building. Since I could barely stand that was not going to be easy.

"There's not enough time for us both to climb down," said the genie. "You go first. Leave the guard to me."

My head exploded with dizzying fear. Did a genie even know how to fight? Who would need to know how to defend themselves with brawn when they had magic? Fear scratched along my spine.

"But he'll kill you," I protested.

"Leave them to me," Dahvi growled. One snap of his fingers set blue fire crackling on his thumb, but the flame went out quickly.

"No, you can't use your magic." Heat coursed through me the second I touched his arm. "You must save it."

"Go." He pushed me away then tried again and again with the same results.

Damn. His magic was still weak.

Behind him, the guard raised his sword over his head.

Terror ricocheted in my skull as I started for the ladder on the wall. "Behind you."

Fire exploded next to us. Pale-blue smoke fanned outward. Something hissed inside the flames.

My pulse jumped into hyper mode as the source slithered out.

Oh crap. The genie had brought the cobras onto the roof. Six of them!

Startled, I almost lost my balance, but Dahvi caught me. It felt incredible to be close to him again. Even just for a fleeting moment.

"What are we going to do?" My voice scaled three octaves.

The guard came to a standstill. I couldn't blame him. If I were him, I'd let the snakes do his job for him. His husky laugh raked down my skin.

"Master, watch out," warned the genie.

One of the cobras struck at me, and I scrambled backward, hitting the parapet. Dahvi used that inhuman speed of his to yank the snake by the tail and fling it at the guard. The rest of the snakes rounded on the genie.

A strangled cry poured from my mouth.

The genie ignited his magic again. All the cobras burst into flames. The fire combined into a single blaze that jumped back onto the genie's hand.

I glanced at the guard. Two halves of a sliced cobra rested at his feet. Hatred fueled his eyes as he continued his pursuit of the genie and me.

"Dahvi, we have to leave now," I screamed, throwing my leg over the roof's edge.

But it was too late. The guard's sword slashed through the air. Dahvi raised a fist, deflecting the blow. The steel clashed on the genie's wristband. Blue sparks exploded over both of them. The guard jumped back, surprised. When he regained his senses, he continued his swipes, forcing the genie backward. The guard grunted as if he'd never had to work so hard to apprehend a criminal. Most probably surrendered at the sight of his sword.

I flinched at every strike. My stomach turned to a sloppy

mess.

"Get down here," someone shouted from below.

Shish kebab. Another guard.

Just because we didn't have enough problems, the third guard stumbled onto the roof from the opposite end.

"Dahvi, we have a problem," I warned.

Blue flames erupted on Dahvi. Out of the resulting swell of smoke came a floating carpet branded with ocean blues and greens.

"I didn't summon you," cried Dahvi, grabbing the sides of his head. "You'll have to do. Get on, Master."

The rug swung over to me.

Little puffs of pale magic extinguished on the silk rug as I put a foot on it. Hundreds of frays spat out from the edges of the carpet, as if it were moulting. Threads of the silk weave unwound and piled on the roof.

"No, no, no," I shouted, grabbing the carpet, trying to stop it from unraveling. It sagged in my grasp as if all of its magic had drained away. I tossed the carpet over one shoulder.

The guard's laugh rumbled in my ear. "What a poor excuse for a genie. I'll be rewarded handsomely when I deliver both your heads to the vizier."

For that, Dahvi punched him in the nose, sending him flying across the roof.

The guard on the ladder grabbed my injured ankle and squeezed. Streams of pain coursed through my leg, and I screeched. Instinctively, I kicked him with the heel of my boot. Blood poured out his nose.

"I'll kill you for that, bitch." His fingers dug into my leg, and I screamed. He tugged at me, trying to pull me off.

"Eat sand," I said, looping both arms through the ladder. This time, I drove my heel into him with more force.

He grunted and thumped me in the thigh.

Gods. I could barely move from the numbing pain. Over

and over, I slammed into him. Nothing worked to push him off.

Bleeding from his forehead now, the fat-bellied pig snatched the carpet from me.

"No." I let one arm go to try to get it back.

The guard sneered.

One end of the magic carpet jolted upright as if sparked back to life. Magical fire blazed across the surface, weaving all its threads back together.

My jaw dropped. Maybe the genie's magic wasn't dead after all.

The guard stumbled down one rung on the ladder. Taking my chances, I thrust my leg at him, connecting with his chest. This time, he fell from the ladder, landing with a thud on the ground below.

I flinched for hurting him. But it was either him or me. And I chose me.

Something whacked me in the side of my face, ending my assault. Pain cracked down the side of my skull. Blinding light blurred my vision.

Someone grabbed me by the armpits and hauled me over the building's edge.

"I've got the street rat," said the voice of the guard Dahvi had been fighting.

Tightness clamped around my lungs. *Oh gods.* Where was the genie? Was he alive?

"Dahvi," I screamed.

Muffled shrieks followed, and the guard's grip on me loosened.

I blinked away the fog in my vision. To my surprise, it was not the genie who was my savior but the magic carpet. It had wrapped around the guard's neck and dragged him backward. The guard scratched at the carpet, trying to get it off his face.

I rubbed my forehead, both in bewilderment and relief.

The magic carpet lifted the guard into the air and over the roof's edge. His legs thrashed, fingers clawed. A smug sense of satisfaction pumped through me as the rug let him go. Several thuds and a scream sounded as he crashed below.

Two down. One to go.

My heart hammered into overdrive.

On the roof, Dahvi fought the last guard with his fists. The genie took a blow to the gut and chest. In return, he unleashed an elbow into the guard's face. Dazed, he sank to his knees. The genie snatched the guard's sword from his grip and cracked the man on the head with the hilt. The guard slumped to the ground like a sack of spices.

Three down.

"Dahvi," I said, stumbling back onto the roof.

His chest heaved as he rushed to me. "Master." He pulled me into his arms and held me tight.

I pressed my head to his shoulder, listening to his quaking heartbeat.

"Did he hurt you?" He smoothed hair from my face.

"No. But another guard tried to pull me off the ladder." I wanted to say more, but when I lifted my head, I got lost in the stormy sea that was his eyes. Fireworks popped in my chest. I'd never had anyone come to my rescue before other than Karim. Something about having a guy protect me for once made me feel amazing.

"I've lost count of the number of times I had to jump in and help Kaza out of a tussle," he said with a chuckle, squeezing me tighter, filling me with his delicious warmth.

So that's where he'd learned to fight. I imagined Kaza getting into a lot of trouble with his flirty winks.

"And not a scar on you." I poked Dahvi's nose and giggled.

"Are you saying I fight like a girl?" He tickled me.

"No." I squealed.

Suddenly, I was overwhelmed with the urge to kiss him. But as we both leaned in, something jabbed me in the butt, and I accidentally head-butted him. Rubbing my forehead, I glanced over my shoulder. The cheeky rug waved a tassel at me.

"Sit," said Dahvi, taking my hand and helping me onto the carpet. "Take the weight off your foot."

I'd always been the one responsible for Ali. Getting his medicine, clothes, water and food, cooking, cleaning, and washing. I really liked the way Dahvi fussed over me. Having someone take care of me for a change was refreshing. This was something I could get used to.

Once I was comfy, Dahvi dragged one of the guards over to the rug and lifted him on.

"What are you doing?" I scrambled to the farther edge, terrified he'd wake up and try to kill me again.

"We can't leave them here." Dahvi went back for the other guard on the rooftop. "When they wake, they will return to the vizier with news of finding us. That will leave our brothers in danger."

Smart. I can't believe I didn't thought about that. My mind still hadn't caught up with all the complications in my life and my lack of sleep. All of this had left me exhausted. I needed sleep desperately. Gods! I probably looked a sight with dark bags under my eyes. Being around someone as sexy as Dahvi wasn't helping either. I could barely concentrate on anything besides those eyes.

For a few moments, he took my hand and massaged the joints. "We'll take the guards and leave them a few days' march from here."

Nice. That head start would give the genies time to recover. A chance for me to save my brother. *Gods.* So much responsibility again.

I patted the carpet. "I have just the place."

"Where's the last guard?" asked Dahvi, scanning the rooftop.

"In the alley," I said.

My muscles braced for a bounce as he jumped on beside me. But the carpet didn't budge. Only the tassels jiggled in the breeze.

A squeal burst free as the carpet sailed over the edge of the building and lowered us into the alley, the walls of which had been covered in graffiti from the local children.

Dahvi tiptoed around the plants potted in wine barrels to lug the final guard onto the carpet.

With a smile, Dahvi pulled me between his legs and snuggled me, my back to his rock-hard chest. Basking in his warmth, I nestled into him, feeling so secure.

His breath feathered my neck. "Where to now, Master?"

My belly bubbled with excitement. I was about to go on a magic carpet ride! "Head east for the lands known as The Den. Then we'll take a detour to visit my friend Scarlet in the woods of Terra."

Dahvi whispered to the carpet in a foreign language that sounded like pure magic. The carpet soared above the apartment blocks.

My stomach sank into my toes. Soon, the sand-drenched alley lay several hundred feet below. Dizziness struck me. Caves and gates, I could handle with no problem. But ridiculous heights like this weren't my thing.

His lips grazed my ear, and my heart trotted like happy, Arabian horses.

"Look, Master." He pointed downward.

Water roared in the fountain at the center of Utaara, which fed the lush gardens filled with hedges, crawling, flowering vines, roses, and fish ponds. The carpet shifted left around tiled archways and monuments. Brightly colored silk awnings and citizens wandering the cobbled streets all contrasted with the sunbaked orange buildings.

I gasped, and my hand flew to my chest. Such beauty I'd never seen before. This was perfect. I leaned even harder into him, and he held me tighter. Being next to him felt incredible. I'd always imagined strolling through the lanes of Utaara, hand in hand, with someone special. Leaning my head on his shoulder. Having his comforting arm around my waist. Feeling safe, loved, and supported. Dahvi stirred those feelings inside me, which was insane, considering I hardly knew him. Yet he'd done something to my insides I couldn't explain.

The magic carpet peeled west, heading along the sultan's road, leading out of Utaara. My heart bounced in my chest at the thought of seeing my friend Scarlet. With Ali so sick lately, I hadn't seen her in over a month, and I longed to talk to her, get a new batch of tea for Ali, too.

Dahvi's head pressed against the back of mine. "Utaara reminds me a little of the deserts back home. Tell me about this Terra land. Exploring new places is a hobby of mine and part of the job."

"Me, too." I twisted to look at him, impressed we had something in common. My line of work often called for me to steal artifacts and treasures and exchange them in other realms of Haven. But...at the end of the day, I did not belong to a lamp and a master. The thought of having to eternally serve new masters made my chest ache.

The genie laughed, deep and hearty, and the sound lightened my mind. "My mother used to say curiosity always led me astray."

"So did mine." I smiled, remembering driving my mother batty when I disappeared all the time to explore Utaara.

By the time I was five, I'd memorized the entire map of Utaara. I knew every nook of the slums' alleys. I'd snuck into the palace seven times and pinched countless fruit from the gardens. In the last four years, I'd visited four of the seven realms of Haven. Terra, for Ali's herbs from my friend Scarlet. The Darkwoods, to trade with the merchants. One time, I had trekked to the mountains in White Peaks, but it was too cold for my blood, and I never went back. But the one place I kept returning to was Wildfire by the beach. A few times, I'd taken Ali when he was well. We'd swum, caught fish, and ate enough bananas and mangoes to make us sick. Every time, we'd hoped to see the merfolk who lived underwater in Tritonia, but we were never lucky enough.

My heart craved adventure and endless possibility. But my circumstances with Ali and our finances didn't often permit travel. In Dahvi, I sensed a kindred yearning for journeying.

"Terra is sublime," I began, finally answering his question. "Covered in thick forests, streams, and brimming with every herb imaginable. That's why my friend lives there." I tucked my head. "That probably doesn't compare to what you've seen."

"I have seen many lands." His voice held a rueful quality. "One of pure darkness and terrible beasts. Wastelands of ice. A land so barren and dead that the people lived underground."

My mind soared at those new possibilities. Perhaps once everything was dealt with, I could take the genies and Ali exploring around Haven.

"What's it like in your world?" I asked as the carpet bumped on a pocket of air, and I gripped Dahvi's leg.

"Tribe Marid, where I come from, is a paradise." He used his hands to express himself, and I watched their fluidic movement entranced. "Water and rock pools, tropical vegetation, homes beneath the water, and camps above land."

It sounded like heaven, and I longed to visit there. "Can a

human travel there?"

"No." He ran a hand down my arms, and my skin sparked with blue-genie magic. "Only those touched by the gods' magic, those bearing the mark, may cross the barrier between our worlds and survive."

Oh. Well, that sucked then. Wasn't fair that genies could live and visit our world, and we were not permitted to enter theirs.

I left a hand on his thigh, and it sizzled from the heat raging between us. "Are Zand and Kaza your brothers?"

"No," replied the genie. "But we are family now."

That made sense. Kaza had said the genies were considered traitors to their kind and banished from their home world. So they only had each other now. My heart squeezed for them.

"What is Zand's and Kaza's home like?"

"Zand's hometown is full of fire," said Dahvi, his hand panning the expanse of sky. "Volcanoes, fiery pits, lava, heat-tolerant plants."

Wow. I tried to picture that. The place sounded pretty chaotic. Perhaps it was best humans couldn't visit. What if a ball of lava exploded on their head?

"Kaza's land...well." Dahvi laughed. "It hovers in the clouds. Everything is light and airy, and everyone farts."

We both laughed at that. Correction—I snorted. Gods. I shrugged.

Dahvi gently squeezed my shoulders, easing the tension. "Will you get some herbs for your brother in Terra, too?"

Whoa! Way to ruin the perfect moment.

I cleared my dry throat. "Ali needs dragon's thistle oil, one of the strongest herbs in the land, but it is so expensive, not even my friend Scarlet can get her hands on it without payment upfront."

Dahvi stroked my arms. "Your brother is a kind soul. I

will miss our chats when I leave."

The way he said it made it sound as if the situation between us was strictly a business deal. As if I was nothing more than a customer he was bound to serve. My chest tightened with confusion.

When I'd released the genies from the lamp, I'd felt a tug on my heart, a connection, as if the genies and I were linked somehow. Gods. I was so stupid. I'd misread everything. Dahvi was just touchy-feely. He liked to give people massages and hugs. No way was he interested in me. Not after I lay with his brother.

My throat stiffened. This was why I never got close to anyone. I never wanted to get hurt again. Other than Ali, I'd never let anyone but Scarlet get close to me. That way, no one could throw us away like our mother had. Yet, the genies did something to me. Cracks had appeared in the walls I'd built around my heart when I met them. Every interaction with them caused more of my barriers to crumble. Pretty soon, there'd be nothing to hide behind. The thought of being left exposed terrified me. And although I'd only known the genies a short time, it felt as if I'd known them a lifetime, and my heart stabbed at the thought of saying goodbye. Even if Dahvi didn't feel the same way.

I took his hand and squeezed it. "I'm very lucky to have found you." My voice cracked a little. "To spend time with you and to get to know you. To me, that is the greatest treasure."

A comfortable silence swallowed us. I liked that we didn't need to speak to enjoy each other's company. That he didn't demand I keep him entertained. That he kept me tight in his embrace. I shoved aside how my future would turn out and stared into the distance at the glorious blue skies, the bright sun beating down on me, and the desert landscape over which we flew.

Some time later, the sun commenced its descent below the horizon. The first star of the evening speckled the darkening canopy above. Shadows stretched across the woods we crossed. Soon, we'd reach Scarlet's shop. But for now, we had guards to dump in the forest of The Den.

"We should fly low and find a tree to tie these guards to," I announced.

The genie whispered to the carpet, and we sailed down, my stomach lurching from the sudden dip. We rushed over a river that transformed into waterfalls. Mist splattered my face, and I smoothed it over my hot neck. We entered the woods, dodging staggering-sized trees, but Dahvi held me tightly as I leaned into the movements. Fallen leaves and logs, clusters of shrubs, and patches of mushrooms and herbs filled the land. This place was heaven compared to the hot, harsh land of Utaara.

Ahead, I found the perfect place to drop the sultan's guards. "What about over there by that giant oak?" I pointed for Dahvi.

The genie commanded the carpet to hover just above the ground. Then he rolled the palace guards off with his foot. They thumped onto the ground in a pile. Once they woke, they could make the trek back to Utaara.

I didn't need to tie them and leave them there to die. Knowing the vizier, he would probably kill them when they returned with news that they had let the genie and me escape.

Dahvi leapt back onto his carpet. "Where to now, Master?"

"Follow the river, and it will lead straight to Scarlet's home in Terra," I said, sitting beside him this time, not wanting to lose myself in his saltwater scent and heavenly arms and chest.

"How did you meet your friend if she lives in another realm?" he asked, taking my hand and massaging my fingers.

Gods. Why wouldn't he stop touching me? It was making it hard for me to think. Just being near him frazzled my nerves. But having him caressing me, too? Damn!

"Years ago," I explained with a moan of pleasure, "the avestan prescribed swallow's nettle for my brother, but the avestan did not have any and told me he would pay me to retrieve some from the woods of Terra."

"Sounds like your medicine man never has herbs," joked the genie.

I laughed at how true it was.

"That's where I met Scarlet," I said, admiring the water cascading over the rocks in the stream. "She was collecting other herbs for her tea mixtures. We got to talking. She took me back to her shop and showed me what to brew for Ali. We've been friends ever since."

"That reminds me of my friend Uruku." A hint of sorrow replaced Dahvi's former cheer. "He loved herbs and spices. Used to make up the best stews. Ahhh. But that was a lifetime ago."

He'd lost the people he loved, too. So had all the genies. A rawness settled into my bones. The unfairness of it all simmered inside me.

"Oh, crap," I said, swiveling on my knees. "We just went past Scarlet's shop. It's back there."

Dahvi called the carpet to arc back, and we ground to a halt right outside the door of my friend's shop. He jumped off first, offering me a hand then lifting me off the hovering carpet.

What a gentleman. My heart lifted at being treated like such a princess.

Cold pricked my arms, and I shivered, rubbing them.

Trees creaked as they sway. Frogs croaked their nighty chorus. It was a perfect symphony.

Paint peeled from the windows of Scarlet's shop, which she called, *Get Your Herb On*. The windows were smudged as if they hadn't been cleaned in a decade. Vines crept up to the walls of the little building. Red letters on the sign dangling over her doorway were faded and needed another coat of paint.

Dahvi offered me a flower from one of the vines. I wasn't sure how to feel about the gesture. He was giving me mixed signals. Earlier, he'd made it pretty clear we were just friends. Giving someone flowers was a romantic gesture. Perhaps the djinn gave flowers to their friendship, also. *Gods!* My head pounded with confusion. I didn't want to think about it anymore.

"Thanks," I said, taking the flower and sticking the stem over my ear.

The lights were off inside Scarlet's shop, so I peered through the front glass door. A faint glow came from the back of the building, telling me she was working late as usual. The illumination revealed rows of shelves, packed with jars of varying sizes.

"Right," I said to Dahvi. "It's time to get your brother out so my friend can see to his wounds."

I glanced around the woods, making certain no one else was around. If the priestess's guardians saw us, they would arrest us for using magic.

Damn it. How stupid of us to fly across Terra on a magic carpet and not watch out for the priestess or her guardians. I wanted to kick myself for being off guard. Blame it on the distracting conversation with the genie. What if we had been spotted and the priestess or her men were on their way to apprehend us now? I couldn't have anything else getting in the way of my plans.

CHAPTER 8

"*W*hatever you do, don't use magic in the store, okay?" I told the two genies staring at me. "Oh, and don't tell my friend you're genies."

"Why?" asked Kaza, breaking off a twig to clean his teeth.

On my last visit, my friend Scarlet mentioned the priestess ruling over Terra dictated everything. She forbade magic, and anyone caught doing it was imprisoned for life. Trespassers from other regions, like us, were considered illegals, so we had to remain discreet and not draw any unwanted attention.

"Magic is banned around here," I said. "Anyone found using it is punished and killed."

Dahvi nodded. "Understood, Master." He got busy hiding the magic carpet behind a bush out front of my friend's store.

Good. *Gods, I loved giving orders!*

Pity Kaza didn't take me seriously, winking at me and puckering his lips in a kiss. Wounded, pale, sweating from fever, and with the gold in his eyes washed out from weakness, he still managed to find the strength to flirt.

Gods, love him…I sure knew I was fond of him.

In his current state, I hadn't wanted to bring him out of the lamp. But I doubted Scarlet would have given me the medicine without seeing the patient first.

I knocked at the door and waited.

Kaza's hands found my hips. His lips pressed against my neck. "Remember last night?"

Heat scaled up my throat and into my face. How could I forget? But did he have to mention it in front of Dahvi?

"Come visit me in the lamp again." Kaza nipped my neck. "Tonght."

Blinding light from the porch suddenly illuminated us, and I snapped to attention. The door creaked as it swung open. A little bell chimed, too.

"Azar?" Scarlet stood in the doorway, wearing a wolf onesie, her hair pulled back in braids. She certainly loved her onesies. Had one for pretty much every animal—bear, rabbit, tiger, owl, cow, bee, and the list went on.

I bounded up the stairs to give my friend a hug. "I've missed you."

Scarlet returned the embrace. "What are you doing here so late? Is Ali okay?" She glanced over my shoulder, scanning the two genies. Her eyes paused on each one.

"Charming outfit," Dahvi said.

I almost melted into a puddle at the sound of his sexy voice.

"Brings out your eyes," agreed Kaza, offering his flirty smile of greeting.

Scarlet's smile cut short as her savvy, crystal-blue eyes drifted down Dahvi and Kaza's bare chests.

Well, heck! If someone showed up on my doorstep with guys wearing pants and vests that revealed their chiseled chests and stomachs, my gaze would be roaming, too!

"What's going on," my friend asked, her tone tipped with curiosity.

Guess me showing up out of the blue with two semi-naked guys was a little unusual. But Scarlet was used to seeing nude people all the time. Some with boils and warts. Others with burns. *Gods.* My brains burned from picturing the sagging, old men she'd probably treated. Good thing I never got into the herbal profession.

"Quick." Scarlet shoved Kaza inside. "Come inside before someone sees you."

I trailed behind Dahvi and closed the door behind us.

In the entry hall, Kaza took Scarlet's pale hand and kissed it. "Why, hello, my master's friend, I am Kaza." He jabbed a thumb over his shoulder. "This is my less-attractive and not-as-funny brother Dahvi."

Dahvi laughed off the jab and bowed.

I nudged Kaza in the ribs. This wasn't the kind of place to be throwing around terms like "master." Not with the priestess and her spies on patrol. We weren't supposed to be here. I didn't want to be caught and imprisoned again for the second day running.

Scarlet shyly brushed aside a lock of dark hair. Her grandmother had raised her to be a real lady. No doubt, I could learn a few things from her.

Kaza gave my bottom a pinch before wandering away with Dahvi to admire the store's supplies.

My boots clomped on the polished wooden floors as I entered the shop ahead of Scarlet. One wall had shelves filled with jars of teas and other dried herbs. The front counter was filled with parcels of healing teas, ready for delivery by Scarlet's assistant I assumed.

Scarlet leaned into me. "Since when do you hang out with two adorable guys? Well, that blond one looks pretty ill; is that why you're here?"

What was she saying? I was a saint who didn't date?

Hmmm. Guess she was right for the most part, but if the genies stuck around, that might change.

Scarlet gripped my chin and swiveled it from side to side. "Look at your skin. It's glowing. You finally took that lavender solution I mixed up for you."

"It's taken away that uptight edge," joked Kaza as he picked up a jar of something that looked like dried weeds.

No. The lavender wasn't the reason for my glow. For that, I owed a big "thank you" for the genies' presence and the amazing sex I had that morning. But I wasn't saying that out loud.

"Listen," I said, trying to get off that topic. "We're here to get some ferret's leaf. Do you have any?"

Scarlet's eyebrows rose. "That's an extremely rare and potent herb. Expensive, too. What do you need it for?"

My gut twisted into knots. Gods. I hadn't even thought about payment. And the less she knew, the better. If the priestess caught wind of our visit and came snooping for answers, I didn't want to leave my friend in any danger.

Scarlet must have read my thoughts in my eyes. "Pay me back when you can, okay?"

Sometimes, she did this for me when I couldn't pay in full, and I repaid her in installments. She was generous that way. Her motto was she'd rather help someone than be rich. Something I was totally down for.

Dahvi' clamped his hands down on Kaza's shoulders and spun him around to show Scarlet the bloodstained wound dressings. "My brother here is injured."

She gasped, and her hand flew to her mouth.

"Tiger scratch, to be precise," said Kaza. "But it doesn't hurt much. I had a good nurse clean my wound and bandage me up." He gave me a wink.

My heart did flips. I'd tend to him any day.

The yellow-vested genie barely limped as he crossed the room, but I caught the shivering racking his body and the grimaces he tried to hide. Ali did the same, trying to play down his illness when he wanted to go out and fish in the river.

"What kind of trouble are you in, Azar?" Scarlet whispered to me. "The only person who own tigers in Utaara is the sultan."

"And the vizier," I added.

Her mouth pressed into a thin line and she nodded. Apparently, may answer was enough to end her questions. While she was aware of my line of work, she didn't always approve but understood it was how Ali and I had survived this long.

Aromas of various herbs hit me. Sweet, bitter, woodsy, spicy, minty, and menthol.

Glass jars on the top shelf clinked as Scarlet shifted them. She hunted through cupboards, removing a tincture bottle, alcohol preservative, a pot, mixing equipment, and a measuring flask.

"Heavens, Azar," she said on her return to her counter. "Your leg is swollen and bruised. Let me get you something for that."

"Twisted it," I answered.

Scarlet gave me a fierce look that told me she was very worried before she got busy preparing the mixture. She sprinkled all sorts of herbs into a pot with water, along with three drops of a brown liquid. While this boiled on a fire stove in the back corner, she measured out preservative in a tincture bottle.

I helped her, readying a gauze to drain and extract the liquid. I knew how to do these things after I'd watched her do them before, and she'd taught me how to create some brews for Ali.

Unable to keep his hands to himself, Kaza trailed his

fingers along the many jars and sprigs of dried herbs tied in bunches. "Look, Brother," he said, pointing to a water jar with a hose and suction pipe. "A hookah!"

"Scarlet," said Dahvi. "May we try your tobacco?"

"Sure," she said, measuring out some spoonful of herbs onto a set of scales. "Help yourself."

I loved her for that. She was always so generous. I gave her hand a squeeze.

She smiled and put a pot of water on to boil. "When this boils, make yourself a tea with this mixture. It'll reduce the swelling and pain in your ankle. You should be healed in a few days rather than weeks."

Wow. Anything to help me out was a blessing. "Thank you, my dear friend." I gave her a quick hug.

Kaza's yellow magic lit the tobacco inside the glass base, and it bubbled away in the gently boiling water. Smoke curled from the base into the pipe with the mouthpiece, from which he took a long inhale. The air filled with the scent of apricot and vanilla. Shapes formed in the smoke he exhaled. Roses, flying carpets, a genie lamp, necklaces, a pair of lips that puckered as if kissing. But when an erect penis sailed right past me, I snorted and slapped him in the arm.

"You know you love it, my desert queen," Kaza said.

Yes, I did. But he was going to get us in trouble. Displaying magic like that in the open was going to give them away. And in Terra, of all places! The one land where magical creatures weren't welcome.

To my great relief, Scarlet hadn't noticed a thing, her concentration buried in the brew she prepared. Thank gods, too. She probably would have had a heart attack at the penis-shaped smoke.

Gods. I imagined Scarlet's grandmother glaring down at me from the heavens for bringing such filth into her former home!

Kaza took a few more puffs from the pipe, activating a fiery glow in his arm veins and in the golden rings around his eyes. Something told me he couldn't help it. His heart told me the smoke called to the fire within his genie blood.

The knowledge didn't stop me from going into panic mode. I darted in front of Kaza and tapped my foot, hoping my friend wouldn't notice.

"You like my cured tobacco?"

I almost yelped at Scarlet's question.

"Delicious," Kaza said, handing the pipe to Dahvi. "Just as good as the tobacco back home."

My heartbeat thundered in my ears. This was getting too close for comfort. I mouthed the words "no more magic" to Kaza.

Scarlet stirred the bubbling brew, fanning the sickening smell of the herbs my way, nauseating me more.

"Folks come from all around to buy my products," she said.

At this announcement, the genies exchanged impressed glances.

"My tobacco has five hundred five-star ratings on Terra's Customer Approval Plank," continued Scarlet. "Well, until lately, when this disgruntled customer gave me five one stars, and my rating dropped."

"Did she say star gazing?" Dahvi asked Kaza.

This earned a giggle from Scarlet. "You're not from around here, are you?"

"No," said Kaza. "We're from—"

"Come and rest, Brother." Dahvi curled his arms around his Kaza's shoulders and dragged him to the waiting room.

Talk about scaring the hashish out of me.

"Who are those guys?" Scarlet's eyes drilled into mine for an explanation of everything. "They're kind of strange."

I needed an excuse and fast. "They were prisoners like

me." I laughed nervously. "Locked away for a while. Sent them a bit loony. We escaped the vizier together."

Okay. So that was partly true. My friend didn't need to know any more. Her safety depended upon it.

Scarlet took my hand. "Are you in trouble, Azar?"

I squeezed her hand. "A little. Nothing I can't handle."

The bridge of her nose creased in a way that screamed concern. "Do you need any money?"

"No." I waved her away. "You've done enough for me. Let's just say in a week, I'll be able to pay you everything I owe you."

The worry in her eyes refused to leave, even as she continued with her brew.

The water in the pot had boiled, so I left the room to grab a mug from her kitchen out back. Upon my return, I poured the mixture and water into my cup. It steamed in my hand, and I left it to cool. It smelled bitter and disgusting. But if it helped my leg, I'd take it.

I sat on a stool at the counter, waiting for Scarlet to finish Kaza's ointment. It felt good to relieve the ache in my ankle.

"Can you call your friends?" Scarlet asked some time later, holding a jar full of reddish ointment.

"Kaza," I said. "Your medicine's ready."

The genies bustled back into the room.

Don't ask me why, but Kaza, Mr. Show Off, felt it necessary to strip off his vest for its application, even though his wound was on his leg. I laughed into my hand at him.

"Lie on the sofa there," Scarlet said. "On you side."

Kaza groaned as he followed her instructions.

"Sorry, this might hurt a bit," Scarlet explained as she patted a soaked gauze along his lesion.

"Nothing hurts me," said Kaza, blowing me my hundredth kiss.

Gods. If only I could smooch him for real.

Poor Scarlet looked as if she had trouble concentrating. Her gaze kept flickering across Kaza's back. She seemed to take her time in applying the ointment, as if she were dragging it out.

Didn't blame her in the slightest. Taking a sip from my mug, I admired every line of his incredible body. The curve of his rock-hard chest. Rippling muscles across his back. Grooves in his collarbone and shoulders. The perfect specimen. All the genies were.

"This might leave a scar," Scarlet warned Kaza.

I didn't mind if his skin was marked by the tiger's claws. It gave him character. Like the scar I'd received on my arm from the ruthless orphanage operator who'd flung me into a wall when I had refused to be his slave.

"I'd get injured a thousand times for my master." Kaza threw in a wink.

I wouldn't let anyone go through this again. Not for me. I wasn't worth it.

But secretly, a part of my heart soared at Kaza's words. Thanks to our imprint connection, I knew he was being serious and speaking the truth.

Scarlet gave us both an inquisitive look.

I returned it with an *I'll tell you later* glance and took another gulp of my disgusting tea.

When my friend finished administering the ferret's leaf mixture, she looked to me and then back to Kaza. "Something's wrong. The moth's eye and owl's claw should have reduced the inflammation and swelling. The tiger lily should have sealed up the wound by now."

I jumped to my feet. My mouth turned to sand. Why wasn't it working? What was wrong? Was he going to die? At that thought, my knees almost collapsed on me. I leaned against the counter behind me.

Golden sparks flew off Kaza's wounds.

Oh crap.

Scarlet stepped back all of a sudden. The tub of ointment crashed to the floor, some spilling on the leg of her onesie. "Magic," she sputtered.

Kaza twisted around and pressed his finger to her lips. "Shhhh."

My heart exploded. Now we were in deep crap.

Scarlet turned to me. She seized my forearms and squeezed hard. "Tell me what's really going on, Azar, or I can't help you."

I pulled Scarlet into my arms to comfort her. Everything poured out of me—the entire story. From Ali's illness, to the sultan's cave, to the genie lamp, being imprisoned by the vizier, and how the genies had rescued me from the tiger pit.

"Heavens." Scarlet paced along her floor. Her fingers trembled as she rubbed her forehead. "Give me a minute." She took a few deep breaths.

When she returned, I ran a hand along her back.

"Surely, there is an answer in one of your books," suggested Dahvi.

"Books." Scarlet jabbed a finger at the ceiling. "Yes."

She scurried over to her herb book and flicked through it. "Heavens no. That won't do. Hmmm. No." She turned a few more pages, her eyes scanning the text.

My stomach tumbled like a rock rolling down a hill. I glanced at my genies.

Dahvi bit his lip.

Sweat dripped off Kaza. Despite all the kisses and bravado, he was not doing do well.

"This might work," said Scarlet. "The magical sands of Katar was reported to have once healed an injured unicorn."

"Where do I find the sands?" I asked.

Scarlet rubbed the back of her neck. "The Collector trades magical items. She might have some."

The Collector? That bitch didn't exactly have the best reputation. She probably knew of a way to steal my genies, and while my body rotted in some shallow grave, she'd sell them to the highest bidder. My chest threatened to burst at that idea. I couldn't lose the chance to save my brother. Lose the chance for a better a life. Lose the chance to be with them all.

Bitter tears stung my eyes. "No," I said. "No way."

"Red is the only one who can help," Scarlet urged. "She's helped me out a few times."

So The collector went by the name Red huh?

"Master," said Dahvi, his voice insistent and firm. "We must do this."

Kaza's muscles quivered from pain, and he bit his lip. How much longer did he have before his conditioned worsened like Ali's had?

I'd do everything in my power to help save Kaza, as I intended to save my brother. "Looks like we are paying The Collector a visit."

CHAPTER 9

"*Y*ou're not leaving now, are you?" Scarlet asked, grabbing my elbow.

"I'm so sorry. I can't waste a minute. I need to help my brother." Plus, every second counted as Kaza got sicker, too. "I promise my next visit will be for a week." I didn't have the time to spare right now.

Scarlet rubbed her arms. "You don't want to be traveling through the Darkwoods at this time of night. It's home to the tiger shifters. And The Collector has lots of other animals patrolling her borders."

An iciness trickled down my neck. Hmm. Now that Scarlet mentioned those dangers, I was suddenly overcome with extreme exhaustion and needed rest. I'd had enough tigers to last me a lifetime, thank you very much.

"That won't be a problem," said Dahvi, placing his fingers to his lips to whistle.

"Yeah, we have flying carpets," added Kaza.

I squeezed my bag to my stomach, and the lamp inside it jabbed me.

Scarlet looked at me with wide eyes crammed with curiosity. "A magic carpet exists? And you went for a ride?"

Ugh. Guess I had to confess or tell her something. I sighed and said, "It's amazing soaring over the lands. Oh, the view!"

She squeezed my hands and bounced on her feet. I gave a half smile, not sure what else to say. Sometimes, the truth was the easiest solution. Even if it was more complicated.

"Are you up for a moonlight spin?" asked Kaza with a waggle of his eyebrows.

"No," we both barked.

"Evil priestess in Terra," I said to jog his memory. "No magic, remember? No putting my friend in danger."

"That's right." Kaza took a jar of licorice from a shelf and helped himself to a piece. "This land must be so boring."

Scarlet's hands flew to her hips. "That'll be one silver markos, thank you."

Kaza kept chewing. "Don't suppose you'll accept a magical spell I.O.U.?"

I snorted. Over the years, I'd probably accumulated dozens of I.O.U.s to Scarlet. I was glad she was so generous.

Kaza wrapped a clammy arm around me. "You're very, very sexy when you snort, Master." His hands ran along my curves and even cupped my ass.

Flames claimed my cheeks, and I pulled away. Why did he keep teasing me about that? I swatted his hands away. "Not now!"

Scarlet ignored the genie and squeezed my hands again. "Stay the night and leave at first light. You can have Grandma's old room."

Thank the gods! I could do with a proper mattress and pillows. My ankle needed a rest after all the action of today. So did my body and mind. I was confident Zand would keep my brother safe for one night. Worry gnawed at me that they might worry if I was gone for too long.

"Thank you," I said, hugging my friend, adoring how she smelled of citrus.

"Excuse me a moment," said Scarlet. "I'll get you clean bed sheets."

When Scarlet was out of earshot, Kaza nudged Dahvi in the ribs. "Kinky, Brother. We can lay with the master. Though I'm not sure I'd call having sex with her in a grand-mother's old, mothball sheets a turn on."

"Hey, keep your voice down," I said. "No one is having sex tonight." *Gods.* My whole body burned. I wanted him to get in the lamp and stop embarrassing me.

Kaza rolled his eyes.

"Scarlet's grandmother passed away not long ago," I whispered.

Dahvi shoved Kaza in the chest for me. "Brother, show some respect!"

Kaza grabbed my hand and placed kisses along it and up my arm. "Please, accept my humblest apology."

My inner arousal stirred. Gods, he left me burning up!

He nuzzled my neck. "Master, I was only joking. I'm a Shaitan djinn. Fun is in my nature." He squeezed my bottom again, soft then harder.

"Don't worry, Master," said Dahvi, pulling away his brother. "I will not try anything inappropriate with you."

What? No! Secretly, I wanted Dahvi to try everything inappropriate with me, but not tonight. Every part of me ached for his hands to explore my body. Having the two of them explore me made me want to explode with excitement. But I wasn't about to admit that now, was I? The moment wasn't appropriate.

I rubbed my temples. What were these genies doing to me? Turning me into a wild, horny beast? I swore they'd leave me starved for sex when they left.

"Brother, don't play all innocent," said Kaza. "I've seen the way you swoon over the master."

Dahvi tucked his hands under his armpits, highlighting the lines of his biceps. "And I don't deny it."

"I'll just make myself scarce and return to the lamp then, hey, Brother?" Kaza got to his feet, straightened his vest, and patted Dahvi's chest. "Let you two *get acquainted*."

What was he doing?

Yellow smoke swirled around him. He blew me a cheeky kiss before dissolving into it, the vapor streaming into my bag.

Dahvi and I just stood there like two shy teens set up on a date.

Crap. Well this was awkward.

"Brothers." Dahvi shrugged.

The creak of the wooden floor told me Scarlet was on her way back, so I smiled when she appeared armed with a set of sheets and pillowcases.

"Where's the flirt?" she asked, handing the items to Dahvi.

I stroked my bag. "Back in the lamp. Staying out of trouble."

Part of me wanted to strangle Kaza for being so forward with Dahvi and me. Maybe it was a brotherly thing. You know, looking out for his brother, putting in a good word with me. But if Kaza's heart had bonded with mine, why do such a thing? Was sharing women something genies did in their culture?

I hated to admit it, but some part of me kinda liked his brand of trouble. Made me feel alive. Kept me on my toes because I never knew what to expect. Maybe I should take more of a page out of Kaza's book and not be so serious or end up grouchy like Zand.

"Thank you again, my friend." I smiled at Scarlet and

followed her down the hall and into a large bedroom with Dahvi.

"Good night," Scarlet said. "The bathroom is just across the hall, and the kitchen is stocked with food if you get hungry." She winked and vanished into the dark corridor.

"Thank you."

The genie shut the door behind us.

Queasiness filled my belly. Was it true that Dahvi had a crush on me? Or had Kaza been joking around again? Gods, I hoped not. An excited tremble coursed through me at the prospect of lying in Dahvi's arms. I felt giddy, like it was my first love all over again. But if the blue genie was shy, would anything happen between us?

Damn. How could I be thinking this when I'd just said no one was having sex? What was happening to me? Instead of thinking about getting to know him, I jumped straight to the dirty stuff. I was so destined for the pits of hell.

Was it so wrong of me to have a strong attraction for the three genies? The people of Utaara would expel me from society for my behavior. But I didn't care when I couldn't control my attraction, my emotions. There was something between the genies and me. A connection. An unexplainable lure. We'd all felt the pull on our hearts the moment they'd smoked out of their lamp. Whatever that represented, I craved more and to explore what it meant.

Dahvi examined Scarlet's grandmother's old room, prodding a crocheted blanket across the bedside chair.

An old quilt with patches of pink was folded on the end of the bed. Various quilted pillows rested against the headboard. Kaza hadn't been kidding when he'd joked about the mothball smell. Floral-patterned wallpaper was marked with the stains of age. Eyes on a creepy painting of some religious woman, whom I assumed was the priestess, watched my every move. I pulled it off the wall and turned it over.

The genie and I got busy making the bed. I showed Dahvi how to put on the sheets. His side ended up with heaps of creases, but it wasn't a bad effort for his first time.

Dahvi turned to me and brushed a thumb under my eye. "Master, you look so tense. It hurts my back, looking at you. Come. Sit."

He led me to the bed, and I sat on the edge.

Resting on his knees, he took my foot, inspecting my ankle. His fingers worked their magic on the sole of my foot, easing tensions I hadn't known I had.

"Do you ever want to start life again?" I asked.

"I wish for freedom every day." A rueful edge clung to his words as his thumbs pressed deeper into the pads of my feet.

I could relate. We were both victims of circumstance. Him, trapped by a spell that had bound him to a lamp and countless masters until he was freed. Me, a product of my environment and the family into which I was born.

"Do you believe I am the master who will grant your freedom?" I said, drowning in calm.

"Yes," he said as he worked his way up to my ankle and heel.

Gods. No pressure, or anything. The poor genies had been used and abused as slaves. I was not going to be the next asshole. Now, I had to live up to my own promise to free them. As long as they helped my brother…

Curiosity burned inside me, and I couldn't stop the flood of questions. "What will you do when you are free? Visit the universe? Climb the highest mountain? Explore Haven?" Of course the last question was an intentional fishing expedition.

He inched over my pants to my calves, relaxing a really tight muscle. "If I am freed I will lose my powers. I guess I will wander and explore these lands."

My heart broke for him. I could barely breathe over the

ache in my chest. The genies' situation made me wonder what I would do if I were in the same position. I couldn't imagine what it would be like, stuck in a strange land without all the glorious power I used to possess. But it would give me the chance to start a new life in a different land. If Ali and I got a fortune from the genies, I planned to settle by the sea. Maybe Dahvi and his brothers could tag along if they needed a place to stay. Who was I kidding? I'd love to have them. Taking them in seemed fair in exchange for their gift of wishes to me. Especially if they were unable to create a home of their own.

Dahvi's brown eyes, lined with a ring of aqua flecks on the outside, locked on to me. "Unless I meet someone I want to share my life with."

Heat flushed across my face. Did he mean it? Sure, there was an attraction between us, but we hardly knew each other. Maybe he just wanted to get to know me and explore the possibilities. *Gods.* I admitted I was eager to investigate them, too. But my heart contracted, reminding me of the pain I'd suffered over those I'd loved. My deadbeat dad had left my mother to raise me. Ali's father never even knew my brother was born. Raising two children alone had been too much for my mother, and she had left us. The one time I opened myself up to love with a man, he had cheated on me, and broke my heart. I didn't want to get hurt anymore.

I tried to pull my leg free, but Dahvi's grip was firm, so I stayed where I was.

"That's amazing," I moaned.

He pressed his thumbs deeper into my calf. "You're welcome," he replied with a smile more delicious than baklava.

His gaze skimmed over me as if he memorized every inch of me.

An immense, warm wave washed over me. I'd never had

anyone care for me the way Dahvi did. From his massages, to checking on my ankle, protecting me from the guard, and even to caring for my brother. Then there was the way he tended to Kaza and had a natural connection with Ali.

This was the kind of guy…genie…I could fall for if I wasn't careful.

"Mmmmm…do you do this to all your masters?"

"No." Dahvi laughed, deep and honeyed, stoking embers burning within me. He dug into the edges around my knee.

"Don't stop," I moaned as my tension spilled free.

"I'm not."

The kiss he left on the top of my foot set me alight. His grin promised me heaven, and I drifted toward it with abandon.

"Gods," I said on a sigh.

I bit my lip as Dahvi broke up the knots surrounding my knee, giving me both pleasure and pain, both of which I enjoyed.

I really needed this. More than anything. I wasn't lucky enough to get a daily massage from my servants like all the fat cats in Utaara, so this was a rare and blissful gift. One I accepted with open arms and heart. And having a gorgeous genie for my masseuse only added to my enjoyment.

"You carry a lot of tension, Master." Dahvi's vigorous fingertips dissolved a nodule on the top of my thigh, and my muscles tensed from the pain.

Hell, yeah, I did. He would, too, if he had the stress I had on my shoulders.

"I'll get rid of it all for you," he promised, running his thumbs up and down the outside of my thigh, easing the burn scaling through me.

Gods. I wasn't going to say no. Right then, I'd let him do anything to me. Anything! His touch had my center blazing, and I groaned. Need shuddered through me. The apex between my legs grew wetter with desire. I wondered how much better the massage might feel with him touching my bare skin.

He rose off the floor onto his knees, exposing the bulge in his pants. He wanted me, too. His breathing quickened. A deep groan rumbled in his throat. The way he drank me in made me even hotter with anticipation. He hooked his hands onto the back of my knees, dragging me closer so my butt rested on the edge of the bed.

I sat up to stroke his penis. "I want you."

"Your wish is my command."

My heart raced as his hands slid over my his and belly. His eyes drilled into mine as he lifted my kaftan and eased off my underwear. I could barely breath as he tossed them aside, and a chill captured my bare legs.

My doubts kicked in. Was it wrong of me to want this stranger? After I'd had his brother? Did he think any less of me because of what I'd done with Kaza? At that moment, my lust kicked my doubts aside and took control. She wasn't up for questions or second-guessing my actions.

My core tightened in excitement. I ached for him to kiss me.

From his position on the floor, he parted my legs and lifted them over his shoulders. I gasped as he buried his face between my thighs. My nails scraped along the quilt as his tongue flicked my folds. Quivers rocked me as he lapped at my slickness. He gave me an approving moan as if he liked what he was doing.

"Dahvi," I panted as my body convulsed.

I wanted more. *More. More. More.* My heart cried out for him, like dry soil desperate for a soaking rain.

Each pass of his tongue rocketed me into the heavens. My pussy throbbed. He consumed every last drop of me. Every muscle seized with pleasure as he tipped me over the edge. I belonged to him, and he knew it. He left my body rocking with everything he had to give.

Gods. We hardly knew each other. But I was eager to give myself to him. Damn, those genies' charms. They worked to seduce me, all right.

The bridge of my pleasure intensified, and a scream of ecstasy pressed the back of my throat. But I didn't want Scarlet to hear me. This was her grandmother's room! What might she think of us? I bet her grandma never anticipated hot genie action happening in her dusty, old room! I grabbed a pillow, pressing it to my face, and unleashed my scream as my body shuddered with the orgasm devouring me.

Dahvi pulled the pillow away and licked his lips.

Now *that* was sexy. I wanted to do the same for him. Suck him. Taste him. Swallow him.

I'd been left breathless, and my heart worked overtime to pump the blood from my privates to the rest of my body.

Dahvi's excitement tested the fabric of his pants.

Flames swarmed in my libido, and I propped myself up on my elbows. I gawked as he stroked his cock through the material. Slowly, as if to tease me, he stripped away his pants, doing a little sexy jig and tossing his pants on my head. I yanked them off and threw them aside. My attention focused on his hardness. The thick, swollen head of his cock throbbed, dripping a bead of white liquid. He slowly caressed his shaft for me, and it twitched in his fingers. I could tell he liked to take his time. Build anticipation. Take things slowly. Make it last. He was going to kill me with his sexiness.

I was hypnotized by his motions. All my thoughts trained on Dahvi. Every inch of me trembled with desire to have him inside me. The wait was driving me crazy, and I ached for him.

Dahvi climbed over me. The heavy length of his penis

danced in the air like a magical wand. It jerked as I clasped his shaft with an eager hand. A grunt tore from him.

I yearned to take him into my mouth and make him scream. Passion surged in his aqua eyes, and I answered the call of my senses by licking his waiting tip. He responded by grabbing my hair and pulling me away.

"No," he said as some of his pre-cum dripped on me.

What had happened to my shy, sweet Dahvi?

Urgency pulsed through me. To kiss him. For him to enter me. He enjoyed making me wait, teasing me, which made me want him even more. For now, I was no longer his master. I willingly surrendered to him. Whatever he wanted I was up for it. My body was his.

"Gods, your beautiful," he said.

Lightning bolts flashed through me as he ran his fingers through my hair.

Had he taken a look at himself in a mirror lately?

My fingers found my face. He thought I was beautiful?

He ran his hands over my hips and underneath my ass. His gaze turned me into a simmering puddle. In one quick motion, he flipped me onto my stomach as if I weighed nothing. Those sleek hands of his glazed over my butt like silk sheets. His touch was pure heaven. His fingers grazed my wetness, and he laughed, the sound stoking the fire within me.

"Please," I begged, wanting him to have his way with me before I burst from the pressure of my anticipation.

"Patience, Master," he said, his voice pure sex.

Heat fanned across my body as he spread my legs. His hardness caressed my inner lips, teasing me. Hunger charged through me. I was drowning in his game but loving every second of it. Gods. I might be dripping all over Scarlet's grandmother's quilt. Dahvi better hurry up and take me before I ruined the thing!

To my immense relief, he did just that, easing into me, soft and shallow at first, as if testing me. When I moaned, he pressed deeper.

"I'm not hurting you, am I?"

I laughed. "You're not hurting me enough."

He was longer than Kaza and reached the end of me, stretching me. But I adored every inch of him.

I lifted my ass, meeting each steady thrust. My entire body wanted to be consumed by him. To burn in the heat that poured from him.

The springs in the mattress creaked with each thrust of his strong hips.

To hell with it. I no longer cared if my friend heard. Hopefully she'd be happy for me. I sure as hell know I'd be if she found someone as amazing as Dahvi.

The genie's pace quickened, and I fisted the quilt. With each pound, I gasped for air.

"Gods," I said, meeting each strike, diving into his passion, drowning in it.

His fingers laced with mine as he lowered his stomach to my back, his body slapping mine, harder and faster. I let go, and a second orgasm gripped me. My whole body quaked from pleasure I'd never even known was possible. If only I could remain on this high for eternity.

The walls of my pussy clenched, squeezing him, and he groaned with his own pleasure that pulsed into me. He collapsed onto me, and I melted under the scorching heat he radiated. Our breaths heaved in perfect unison.

Pale-blue flames licked across my arms and hands. My heart thumped under my breastbone.

Dahvi rolled off me, and I rested on my side to face him. My hands found his hard stomach. Blue fire ignited on his chest. I felt a calling within me. Flames lit awake inside me, too.

I was curious to know how it worked. "Did you imprint on me too?" I asked, touching my chest.

Dahvi nodded. "Our hearts are now entwined."

I felt him probe the depths of my soul, like fingers flicking through a book containing all the pages of my life. But when he touched the pain I'd buried, I grew frightened and shut down my side of the connection.

He brushed hair away from my eyes. "Do you want to read me?"

My mind screamed at me to search him back. To discover the life of a genie. Before I could stop myself, I dove into him, peeling back the layers.

Someone had hurt him before. Broken off a commitment of lifelong love. Now, he yearned for someone to fill the void inside him. But, like me, he didn't trust his heart with just anyone. Appreciation spilled through me that he'd entrusted it with me.

"Why did she leave you?" I asked, holding his fiery pendant between my thumb and forefinger.

The genie traced a finger along my navel. "She loved someone else." The agony in his words cut into me like a knife. "We were all hurt by someone. I don't dwell on it. That's in the past."

Maybe I should take a page out of his book. My pain only served to drag me down. I didn't want to end up all twisted and dark like the vizier. But something about letting my pain go, about being naked, exposed, and vulnerable...it terrified me. And I had more than just Dahvi to contend with. I was also bonded to Kaza. At any time, he could split me open, examine my heart, and take me to pieces. Lay me bare for the world to see. I hadn't even shared my soul with Ali or Scarlet. The idea of not being able to hide behind anything made me want to clam up.

Speaking of the Kaza issue...that gnawed at the back of

my mind, too. My fondness for him. My affection for Dahvi. My unexplored attraction for Zand. For wanting to deepen my bonds with the genies deepen. But I had to wonder whether that was possible, given the circumstances. Whatever the outcome, I was up for it and for the promise of more of what the genies offered me.

Dahvi's fingers curled around the back of my neck, pulling me closer. "It is odd in your culture that you lay with my brother and me?"

Heat rose in my cheeks. Damn, this bond thing. Now I couldn't keep anything a secret. "Yes. In Utaara, only the sultan or the rich, fat cats have multiple mates."

Finally, Dahvi kissed me. A long, sweet, and soft touch on my lips. When he pulled away, he said, "It's perfectly acceptable in my society."

Why couldn't Utaara be like that? Everyone chose who they wanted, how many they wanted without persecution or judgment.

"You don't care that I am bonded with Kaza?"

"Not at all." Dahvi's mouth brushed the tip of my nose. "He is my brother. Seeing you both happy makes me happy."

Gods. Well, that was one weight off my mind.

Dahvi crushed me to his chest. His hands cupped my cheek. "You look tired, Master. Please, sleep."

"I'm pretty exhausted, but I want to spend time with you." I lay there, my eyelids growing heavy. I hadn't had a wink in over one rotation of the sun. Everything was finally starting to catch up with me.

The sound of his heartbeat lulled me into oblivion. I'd much rather remain in his arms than face my troubles. There was always tomorrow for that.

CHAPTER 10

*B*ack at home, my troubles came flooding back. Furniture was overthrown. The lamp busted. Cushions tossed onto the floor. A plate smashed.

My heart caught in my throat. Gods! Had the vizier's guards ransacked my place and taken the genie and my brother? Breathing was close to impossible as I tip-toed through the mess that was once my hovel.

"Ali! Where are you?" My voice quivered.

Karim jumped up and shrieked at me pointing to the kitchen counter. His eyes were wide and startled. I crushed him to my chest.

A grunting sound from deeper inside. Hope flared in my chest. Someone was alive. Ali!

On the kitchen floor, I found Zand and Ali in a tangle of limbs, roughhousing, shoving each other, and making guttural noises. Neither of them wore a shirt or vest. Both were covered in a sheen of sweat. Ali had the genie in a head-lock and pinned to the ground.

"Submit. Submit!" my brother yelled and laughed.

"All right, you win," said Zand, his abdomen tight and showing off his abs. "Again."

I glanced at Dahvi, who stood there watched them, running his fiery pendant up and down his necklace, and grinning.

What the heck was going on here? Exactly how long had they been wrestling like this? A rush of panic clawed at my insides. Did the monster of a genie hurt my brother? Ali was in no condition to be messing around. Where had all this strength come from all of a sudden? He'd been so weak for so long. Was the genies' magic somehow breathing new life into my brother?

"What are you doing?" I snapped. "Ali, you're sick. Why aren't you in bed? Who busted up the house?"

Ali and Zand both glanced up and then collapsed onto the floor, laughing.

Karim started moaning nervously in my arms. He always did that when I told him off. The poor little thing thought I was yelling at him. I stroked his head and hugged him.

"I feel better." The cough that followed Ali's words told me otherwise, and I narrowed my eyes in his direction.

"You were gone for a day," Ali said with a shrug as if it wasn't a big deal. "We were bored. Messing around."

Clutching Karim in one arm, I grabbed Ali with the other to check for bruises. "You could have hurt him," I barked at Zand.

"Azar." Ali removed my hands away gently. Our gazes met. Annoyance flickered in his eyes. "I'm not a kid anymore. Stop fussing over me."

My heart sank. He'd never pushed that before. We'd always been so close. He leaned on me. Relied on me. And I him. Now, it felt as if a crack had opened in the ground between us.

Zand gave me a kiss on the cheek before picking up the

shards of broken ceramic from my plates. "We'll fix this in no time. Don't worry."

Heat scaled down my neck.

Damn, that genie. I wanted to punch him right in the nose. My brother could have been seriously injured.

My hands fisted. "You just need to be careful, Ali."

A long cough rocked through him and had me reaching for him.

Zand gave my brother a good thump on the back, as if to help Ali clear his chest. It worked, and my brother stood straighter and smiled.

"Your brother's been cooped up for too long," said the red genie, flicking his long mane over his shoulder. "My mother used to tell my father that a little fun is good for the inner flame. Revives it." He thumped his chest with a fist.

My eyes lingered on the spot where he'd hit himself. I ought to be pissed at him, but damn him and his logic…and his sexy-as-hell chest. Maybe having the genies around served as a good distraction from Ali's poor health.

Dahvi put his hands on my shoulders and squeezed, massaging the taut flesh. I brushed him off and restored the fallen lamp to its original position.

Part of me was joyous that Ali had taken to the genie. He'd always wanted a brother. When Ali was younger, he would play in the streets with the other boys in the slums. As a teen, his health had fluctuated, which had made it difficult for him to keep friends to play with. I guess I was grateful that Zand had entertained my brother. But part of me couldn't get past the bitter sting of Ali's rejection. I couldn't lose him like I'd lost my mother. If I did, I'd have nothing.

Maybe I was being ridiculously overprotective, like a momma bear. Ali was a grown man. In a few years, he'd make a home for his own family. Where would that leave me? A penniless thief and alone.

Ali's muscles shook hard as he righted the tattered sofa with Zand. My heart screamed to go and help him, but my brain told me otherwise. Let my brother be a man.

Karim scrambled from my arms, and leaped onto the sofa where he bounced around. Ali laughed and gave his head a ruffle.

Dahvi tossed some cushions onto the sofa.

"Where's Kaza?" asked Zand as he restored the lopsided cart that made up our dining table. "Did he get his medicine?"

I couldn't utter a word past the hurt still jammed in my throat.

Dahvi answered for me. "The ferret's leaf tea didn't work on Kaza. He's in the lamp."

"Give it to me," growled Zand.

I removed the lamp from my bag, but it zapped me the moment Zand touched it.

The genie cupped the brass object and lifted it to his face. "Don't worry, brother. I'll find a way to save you."

A puff of yellow smoke hit Zand square in the eyes.

"I'll toss you in the flames of noruze for that, Brother." Zand shook the lamp really hard, as if there was liquid inside and he was mixing it up.

Ali bent over laughing.

Kaza yelled something in what I assumed was djinn language. Most likely a curse or something. Served him right. That smoke stank distinctly of fart.

"Gods," said Ali, holding his nose. "That reeks."

"Believe it or not," said Dahvi, opening the door for some fresh air. "That's Kaza's way of thanking us."

That lifted my spirits a little, and I snorted with laughter. Genies had a weird way of thanking each other.

"Sexy, Master." Kaza's discombobulated voice piped from the lamp.

Gods. He was loopy if he thought my snorting was attractive.

"A little taste of his own medicine." Zand smiled, revealing a perfect row of straight white teeth as he farted into the lamp's spout and jammed a finger over it.

A series of pounds on the side of the lamp sounded.

I snorted a laugh again.

"Not funny, Master," Kaza moaned, his voice distant and echoing.

Gods. I was lucky I only had one brother to deal with. A whole household of men meant too much testosterone, and competition stained the air.

I accepted the lamp and returned it to my bag, wondering how Kaza was doing. Was he in pain? Did he need anything? I assumed he would have said something if he was too uncomfortable. But, hey, I wasn't a guy, and I didn't understand the whole tough-act thing.

After that little fart and wrestling exchange, it was time to get serious and plan our next move to get the magical sands Kaza needed before it was too late. Two days had passed since we had escaped the vizier. Time wasn't on our side, and it wouldn't be long before the creep and his guards found us.

"Zand." I grabbed him by the forearm, needing to discuss the next steps. "My friend, the healer, says Kaza needs something called the sands of Katar. Nothing else will heal a magical creature."

Zand loomed over me, sending my pulse into orbit. I stared right into his perfect chest muscles. My tongue itched to lick and bite them.

Gods, woman, control yourself. We have a mission here!

Zand put his vest back on, meaning my eye candy wasn't so visible, and my focus could at last realign.

"Where do we find these sands?" he asked.

Dahvi huddled with us. "We were told a woman known as The Collector in the Darkwoods might possess the sands."

Ali joined us as if he felt left out.

Zand rested a huge arm on my brother's head and rubbed his armpit on my Ali's hair.

Ali hit the genie. "I hate being short," he grumbled.

Boys... I rolled my eyes. Definitely too much testosterone here. That aside, I enjoyed having the genies there. The way they'd turned my brother around, brought him to life—hell, they'd brought light and joy to our entire life. Not to mention all the laughs and my embarrassing snorts, or the mind-blowing sex I'd shared with Kaza and Dahvi.

Zand's eyes narrowed. "Where is this Darkwoods?"

"A day's trek," I replied, using every ounce of control not to grab those huge biceps.

"That's too far for the master on foot with her ankle," said Dahvi.

Damn straight! My ankle still hurt but not as much as yesterday, thanks to the tea Scarlet had given me.

"We'll need the magic carpets." Zand moved away to select one of my shawls from the rack I hung my meager selection of clothes on. He threw the item over his head and torso, as if preparing to leave.

"Can I come with you guys?" asked Ali. "I've never been to The Darkwoods."

Neither had I. Rumors spoke of strange creatures and an evil queen dwelling there.

"Sure," said Dahvi, wrapping an arm over Ali's neck.

"Nooooo." I tried to drag my brother back to his bed by his arm, but he yanked himself free.

"I'm not a kid anymore, Azar," he said, his eyes blazing with a fierceness I'd never seen before. "I'm part of the team, too." A cough stole the rest of his words.

My heart cracked in two. All my brother had ever wanted

was to join me when I stole our dinner. To be part of the action. But he'd always been too sick...and I'd never let him. Now, he wanted to show off in front of the genies. Prove his manhood. But I couldn't risk him getting hurt. The Collector had all sorts of creatures guarding her fortress. Ali was slow and weak. He'd never be able to get out of the way fast enough if a beast tried to pounce on him.

I swallowed hard to dislodge the boulder caught in my throat. "You're staying here. Dahvi, Zand, and I will go get the sands."

Zand retrieved the lamp from my bag and whispered to it, igniting the burning red letters on its surface. His eyes glowed with regret when he glanced at Ali. "Sorry, little brother."

Red smoke poured out of the spout, hooking my brother's arms and drawing him closer.

"No, Zand. Please."

But my brother's pleas did nothing to change the genie's mind. And in an instant, he was sucked inside the lamp. Little puffs of red smoke steamed out, reminding me of an angry bull.

Karim went wild and screamed.

"Shhhh," I told him and he hid underneath a pillow.

"Hey, little brother!" Kaza's said, his voice echoing from within the lamp. "Welcome. Let me show you around. Sorry about the smell."

I snorted as Zand shoved the treasure back inside my bag. My poor brother was in for a treat.

"No," I said to Zand. "We must hide this."

"Why?" His brows pressed down over his beautiful, fiery, brown-and-red eyes.

"The Collector accumulates magical goods," I said. "We can't have this fall into her hands. Otherwise, she will command you."

Zand and Dahvi exchanged glances.

"Very well," said the red genie. "Where can we hide it?"

"Here," I said, crossing the room and shifting the mattress aside to reveal a loose piece of concrete. I stuck a finger under it and lifting it to reveal a cavity I'd hollowed out for items like this.

Zand rested the lamp in the space, and I replaced the concrete to conceal it. "Let's leave at nightfall," he said, taking a seat on my tattered sofa.

"Karim," I said to the monkey. "You guard this. Don't let anyone find it, okay?"

The monkey squeaked his approval.

"Good boy," I said, patting his head.

I sat beside Zand, his breadth squashing my right side against the armrest, but I quite liked him pressed against me. My foot tapped with impatience. What were we going to do in the meantime? I wanted to leave now. Heal Kaza and camp somewhere safe until all the genies' powers were restored.

Dahvi picked up my brother's pack of cards. "A game to keep us busy?"

"Yes, please," I said, rubbing my hands, desperate to distract myself from the task ahead of me.

* * *

THE CRUNCH of leaves and twigs told me my genies were close. Thank the gods. Moonlight failed to penetrate the thickened canopy of The Darkwoods. Eerie shadows reached out for me like a monster's claws. Even with my eyes well-adjusted to the dark, I could barely see a damn thing. My foot rammed into a log, and I stumbled. Zand was fast on his feet and caught me.

I glanced up into his eyes. The red in them flickered. For one instant, I was filled with the overwhelming desire for him to kiss me. But he set me on my feet and kept walking. My shoulders sagged as I continued deeper into the darkness.

We had waited for the cover of night to leave. Not ideal, considering that was probably when most creatures in the Darkwoods came out to hunt, but, hey, the darkness shielded us from any eyes as we'd taken to the skies on Dahvi's magic carpet. Now the rug floated a few feet behind its master.

A glow erupted to my left, casting more shadows across our path. Zand's palms blazed with pale flames. The light wasn't exactly ideal. It was a beacon for all things that went bump in the night. But I didn't like the idea of stepping on something sinister. Rumor had it The Collector had unleashed all sorts of creatures on her land. Poisonous snakes and insects. Flesh-eating unicorns. Blood-thirsty worms that lived underground. This was the one place in Haven that I did not want to step foot on in the dark…or in the light of day for that matter.

But if this trip was going to heal Kaza and help Ali, I'd do it in a heartbeat. I just hoped my heart lasted long enough for me to get in and out of the woods alive with the magical sands we needed.

"Your magic is slowly returning," I said to Zand. "What else can you do?" Behind my question, what I really asked was if he was strong enough to poof me the cash I needed into existence.

Zand brushed a branch away from our path. "I can get us out of here if need be."

That was somewhat comforting, but not the answer I'd wanted.

Something howled and growled nearby.

I spun around, and my shawl fell off my shoulders. My entire body was taut, on high alert. I didn't like this place one bit. Put it down to being seriously out of my element and in strange territory. I shivered from the cool and moist air gripping me like icy fingers. The cooler climate didn't serve me, even if the desert winds at night carried chilled air.

Zand wrapped my shawl back around me.

Having him as well as Dahvi by my side gave me a few extra bars of comfort.

"Thanks," I said, forcing a smile.

Branches grazed my skin like witch's fingernails, and I yelped, bumping into him. He wrapped an arm around me, clutching my waist. Warmth spread through me, chasing away the chill of the forest. The comfort of his arms distracted me from the sudden silence sticking to the air. The shrill cry of crickets, so prevalent a short time ago, had fallen still. All the hooting had stopped. Not even a wind blew, and it seemed as if the trees had frozen in place.

A few birds shrieked. Wings flapped, and leaves rustled as the birds flew off.

My body tensed. Something was wrong.

I screamed and elbowed Zand in the stomach. Normally, I wasn't this flappable, but I felt completely out of my element in the woods.

He didn't so much as even grunt.

"Crap. I'm so sorry." I kissed his free hand.

Growls from the woods slashed through my apology.

I froze.

Zand stood like a bear on hind legs—stiff and ready to attack.

Dahvi held his arms tight to his body, scanning the forest.

A nasty smell washed over me. Fur, dirt, and urine. The marked territory of some animal. Red eyes blinked in the distance amid the trees. Not just one. Six pairs. Judging by the height of their eyes, they stood taller than wolves. Probably deadlier, too, if they had anything to do with The Collector.

"The Collector's beasts," I whimpered.

Zand and Dahvi remained taut and alert.

Claws raked along the ground, the sound of a beast threatening to pounce if we took another step.

A growl rumbled.

Two of the beasts charged. Their pounding footsteps told me they were huge.

I backed up, straight into a tree.

The weak glow from the genie's flame illuminated the attacking creatures. All fangs. Horn for a nose. Clubbed tail with spikes. Covered in hair all but on their back, which was covered by a rock-hard plate.

The animal to the left launched at Zand. He was much faster and dodged the attack, deflecting the beast with a fist to the face. The creature struck a tree and hit the ground with a thud. It whined and stumbled to its feet.

I gasped, surprised that the genies possessed immense strength, too.

The animal limped into the darkness.

My throat tightened. I didn't like seeing any living thing get hurt. But if it came down to my life or theirs, I knew what I'd choose.

The second beast charged.

Dahvi drove the creature back with a punch to its ribcage. Branches cracked from the impact. *Gods,* he was fast.

A short, savage roar exploded from my right. I flinched.

This time, an entire pack of the beasts crashed forward, filling the space between me and genies.

I glued myself to the tree, not moving, barely taking a breath.

The genies delivered blow after blow, repelling the monsters. One bounced across the ground, coming to a stop against a log. Another got launched through the air and stuck in a hole in a tree trunk. A third hung limp from a branch.

The fourth shot straight up and never came back down. This left only one—the largest, most formidable-looking one, which I assumed had to be the alpha. An uppercut from Dahvi knocked it out cold.

"Enough!" said a commanding, feminine voice.

The beasts retreated into the shadows.

I glanced around but found no one.

Zand and Dahvi spun as if they'd heard something I hadn't.

I followed their gazes up into the canopy.

"What are you doing in my land?" Darkness concealed the speaker.

I'd bet my life it was Red, also known as The Collector. My ears pinpointed her location—a branch fifty feet to my left.

It felt like quicksand stuck to the roof of my mouth, and I couldn't get a word out.

Zand took charge of the situation for me. "If you are The Collector, we've come to bargain for the sands of Katar."

A woman dressed in a long green robe stalked farther out along the branch upon which she stood. The bowstring she pulled taut creaked, her loaded arrow aimed at Zand. I wondered if he was fast enough to catch an arrow she launched at him?

What kind of way was this to greet a potential customer who intended to trade with her? Only a crazy person would set their beasts on someone, and then threaten us with a lousy bow. And after what she'd witnessed the genies do? Damn...the girl had some balls. Perhaps she wasn't so willing to negotiate now that my genies had kicked her beasts' asses.

Shock rattled through me like a freight train when the robe slipped from her head, revealing her face. I had expected a hideous hag or worse. But she was the opposite. At about five feet three, she stood a little shorted than me. Red curls cascaded over her shoulders. Pale skin glowed red from Zand's palm fire. Her full lips were the color of roses, and she had curves in all the right places on her toned physique.

Sure, I wasn't bad to look at, with my lean figure and dark features. But this girl was beautiful. I shouldn't be jealous, but that emotion flared awake inside me.

Her posture shifted; she pushed her shoulders back and straightened her neck. "You fools couldn't afford the sands of Katar."

Talk about sassy. Guess you had to be in a career like hers to have such attitude. Add to that little fact that they we were also trespassing on her lands. Guess she had a right to be a bit rude.

"How much do you want for the sands?" I asked.

"Ten thousand markos," she replied.

I almost fainted. Who had that kind of cash? Not even Ali's medicine cost that much.

Zand circled her tree like a tiger sizing up its prey.

Not a hint of fear crossed her face.

"Once you heal our brother," said Zand. "We will pay whatever you ask."

Her green eyes didn't stray from the fire in his palms. Hunger for power rolled in her eyes.

"We pay amply," Dahvi mumbled, his gaze glued to the rise and fall of her perfect breasts.

Fire boiled in the pit of my belly. I'd expect such behavior from Kaza, not Dahvi. But then there was the tiny part of me that couldn't blame him for gawking. Her breasts *were* perfect, and this wasn't the time for me to allow the crazy, green-eyed monster to take over—actually, there was never a good time for that, but especially not now. We had people to save.

The words that came from Red's perfect mouth hit me like a blow to the guts. "Money upfront or no deal."

Just as fast as she had appeared, she vanished into the gloom.

My heart sank to the bottom of my chest. We were screwed. "Let's go," I said and turned around.

But Zand wasn't about to give in so easily. "I have something far more valuable to barter," he called out.

A response from The Collector came out of the shadows. "Oh, yeah? Like what?"

CHAPTER 11

*Z*and whispered in his strange language, and the magic carpet returned, floating a few good meters from The Collector's perch on the tree branch.

The woman's eyes blazed with temptation, and she confidently navigated the limb, balancing on it with ease, as if she'd been climbing her whole life. Reaching out, her fingers traced the length of its silk.

It pulled away as if frightened of her.

"I'm listening," she said to the genie, totally in command of this negotiation.

Zand lifted himself onto the branch beside her. "You can have the carpet and three wishes."

I felt as if a tree trunk had slammed into my gut. I couldn't breathe. Unable to get a word of protest out. What was he doing? Giving away my wishes? How was it even possible for him to leave me when he hadn't granted me a wish? My mind tumbled, trying to make sense of it all.

Red's voice cut through my confusion. "Deal."

My heart crumbled in my chest. "What about the wishes you owe me?"

Zand glanced over at me. "But first, I must fulfill my commitment to my current master."

What? I stared at him, working out his scheme. He was playing the woman. Dirty rascal, and here I thought he was fooling me. I felt like an idiot.

Darkness stormed across Red's face, and she looked ready to spear him in the chest. "Do I look like a sucker?"

She swung around the branch like a gymnast, and landed on the ground with the agility of a cat.

Hands fisted, I jumped in front of Zand prepared to fight for my genies if need be.

Zand sidestepped me, and pulled the ruby ring from his forefinger and held it out for her. "Take this. In one month, my service to my master will be complete. Then you may summon me with this."

Red inspected Zand's belonging as if it were a piece of trash, and her nose wrinkled with disgust. "Prove it."

My hands squeezed by my sides. I couldn't believe my ears. He didn't just ditch me for that prettier bitch did he? "Um, Zand, you got a moment."

He waved a hand at me as if I were a pesky fly. Ruby flames flared on Zand's wrist and jumped onto the ring. They shot out, lashing Red on the wrist, leaving a scorch mark on her skin.

Was he sealing their agreement with magic? What was he doing?

Satisfaction flickered in Red's eyes as she examined the marking. "We are tied magically. Now you cannot cheat me out of our arrangement."

My legs wobbled, and I almost fell to my knees.

The collector accepted his ring with a smile. "It's a deal. Wait here, handsome." Her gaze teased across his body as if she imagined doing the dirty with him. "I'll get you your magical sands."

With a wink, she drifted off into the darkness.

The remaining wreckage that was my heart turned to dust and scattered around my body. That pain twisted into fury. It surged inside me, like a vicious sandstorm blanketing the city.

"I can't believe you've just made a deal without my permission," I shouted. "Aren't I your master?"

"Calm down, Master." He grabbed my hand and stared deep into my eyes. "Trust me. I'm handling it."

I rubbed my forehead. My feet carried me the length between the two closest trees. "I don't understand what's happening here."

"Master if you don't calm down you will ruin everything." Impatience gave Zand's voice a brittle edge. "Control your anger. In this situation it's your greatest weakness."

My ears couldn't believe what I was hearing. Fire scorched the inside of my stomach. I shot him a glare more deadly than a cobra's bite. "I'm helping save your brother so you'll save mine."

Hot, bitter tears streamed down my cheeks. Needing to put space between us, I raced off into the forest. The darkness caught up to me, and I stumbled again on what I thought was a tree root. This brought me crashing down on my knees. I shuffled to sit against a huge trunk, and leaned my head back on it. Dead leaves crunched in my hand, and I let them flitter to the ground, each representing the grains of my heart.

Betrayed thoughts tumbled inside my mind in a thick confusion. Did he not have faith in me to get the sands? I remembered something he'd said to Kaza about stealing all the glory. Was Zand competitive and wanting the triumph? Who cared so long as Kaza's life was saved?

Then there was the issue of Zand leaving me for the collector. Was I not the one who released him from the lamp? Did that not make me his master? What exactly were the rules of the lamp? I hadn't excused him from his service to me. Yet he was making all the decisions for everyone.

Gods. Then there was the selfish part of me, the one that hated to admit, that I was hurt that I had not had the opportunity to explore my feelings for Zand. Maybe I'd fooled myself into thinking that he had an attraction to me too. The tug I and the genies had felt when I released them from the lamp might have meant something completely different to Zand. Perhaps it was gratitude for being freed after so long. Or recognition of the master that would finally free them from slavery. I struggled to process all the thoughts bombarding me.

The crunch of leaves and twigs signaled someone approached.

I wiped away my tears and smoothed my hair.

Please let it Dahvi looking for me. His presence always had a way of calming me. Damn, what I would have given for Kaza to cheer me up with one of his silly jokes.

"Master?" My stomach dropped at Zand's deep voice.

"Leave me alone," I shouted at him.

Flames blazing on his palms illuminated the regret pinching his forehead and the tightness in his posture.

"Please, understand, Master." He put a hand up against the tree I leaned on, filling me with his smoky scent.

I kicked at a log by my foot, refusing to look at him. "That you're leaving me for Red and her goddess curves. Sure, I understand."

Geez. Why was I acting like this? I hadn't bonded with Zand. Yes, I had a crush on him, but that was it. Maybe my chest ached for my brother, for his devastation at losing his new friend.

"No. Never." Zand's voice held a raw edge.

CHARMED

I glared up at him, taking in all his perfect chiseled jaw. "Then what?"

His shoulders sagged under an invisible weight. "Once I became a genie, I was forbidden to ever see my family again."

The torment in Zand's words was like a knife cutting me to pieces. I was bursting to go to him. Take him into my arms. Strip away all his pain. Even though he'd just hurt me. But I was not forgiving him that easily. No matter what my body wanted.

The space where my heart used to sit felt empty and hollow. I could never imagine a life without Ali. I'd be truly lost. I could only imagine a fraction of what Zand must have gone through. What I might experience if Ali died from the black lung. Now, I was beginning to understand Zand much better.

The genie touched his finger where the ring used to sit. "This was a gift from my mother. The only thing left I had to remind me of her. Of home. But I gave it to the collector for my brother, for Ali, for you. I'd never leave you."

My belly stung with the pinch of having misunderstood Zand. No! Not his only treasure. Now in the clutches of that wicked witch, Red!

He got down on his knees in front of me, and I felt a tug in my chest.

"Kaza and Dahvi are the only family I have left," he said his eyes glistening. "I would do anything to save my brothers."

Oh, gods. Zand had sacrificed his freedom for Kaza's life. I pressed a hand to my forehead. What a mess I'd created, only thinking of myself. Zand and I had more in common that I had initially thought. Both of us would do anything to protect our family. Even if that meant giving us the most precious things in the world. This changed things, and made our bond ten times stronger.

I clasped his hand between both of mine. "I'm sorry. I don't want you to lose your brother as much as I don't want to lose mine."

Zand's hands found the back of my neck, lifting my head so our eyes met.

My breaths labored as he kissed away the tears that rested on my cheeks.

"The Collector gave me the sands." He held up a long, thin jar of colored sands. "We should return to administer them to Kaza."

Yes. More than anything I wanted to see Kaza again. For him to make me laugh and smile, and wash away my pain.

"Right now, I just want to be here with you." To kiss away his sorrow and make the most of the month I had left with him before he left my service to work for the collector. I curled his plaited beard around my finger. "At least for a little while longer."

Zand rested the vial at the foot of the tree. Then he seized me in his grasp like a python, never letting me go. Rough and hungry kisses met my lips, and I reciprocated, wanting more. He ran his hands up over my hips and underneath my kaftan, squeezing my breast. Warmth pooled between my legs, and I let out a little moan. Encouraged, he found my other boob.

Passion surged in his eyes, calling me to him. I wanted him as much as I had wanted Kaza and Dahvi. Don't ask me how it was possible, but I did. Despite the fact that I didn't know him as well as the other two genies.

"I want you so much," he moaned, his lips inching down my neck, leaving a boiling trail of pleasure. "I don't want to leave your side."

Grains of my heart began piecing back together. Damn. After what had transpired with the collector, I hadn't expected to hear this. Too many emotions raged within me. Confusion melding with the excitement that he wanted to share me with his brothers. Me! The dirty street rat who came from nothing and had nothing.

"I don't want you to go either." I ran the back of my hand along his strong cheekbones. "You can't lose your new family."

For a moment he turned his face away from me. "Enough about that for now." His voice held a raw edge that sliced me in two. "I don't want to think about it. All I can think about is you."

Powerful hands parted my legs and pulled me on top of his thighs. I gasped, clasping his biceps tight and wrapping my legs around him. Eager fingers knotted in my hair, pulling me to him.

I was a little frightened by the genie's strength after witnessing what he had done to The Collector's beasts. He could tear my arms off if I displeased him. But that power aroused me at the same time. In his presence, I knew he'd never let anything harm me. This notion sent tremors of excitement through my body.

"Let me lie with you." His words promised me paradise if only I accepted.

Neither of the other genies asked my permission. Part of me kind of liked the old fashioned request. My brain screamed at me, reminding me I'd only met the three genies two days ago. Everything was moving too fast, leaving my mind spinning, and unable to catch up. Multiple mates was natural to their culture, but not for mine. Yet I knew with all my being that my attraction to them was more than just lust. It was powerful, thrilling, and all consuming. Just one look and I was theirs. The though of losing any one of my genies made it unbearable to breathe.

Regardless of what my mind said, the pulsing warmth and wetness between my legs did not care one bit. Each of the genies fit a niche within me. Kaza for uplifting my spirit.

Dahvi to bring me comfort. Zand to protect and look after my brother and me. More than anything, I wanted to bond with him and make him part of my heart, too. Make them all a part of me and I of them.

To hell with what my brain said. Tonight, I was following my heart.

"You have my permission to lie with me." I yanked off his vest and tossed it aside. Biting my lip, I let my fingers explore the hardness of his chest and stomach. He groaned at my touch, urging me to search further, and I ran my hands over his arms and shoulders. "Gods you're huge."

"Runs in the family." The wicked look he gave me told me I was in for a lot of trouble…of the good kind.

He lifted my arms above my head and held them there with one hand. His grip on me was firm, unrelenting, telling me he was the boss. Of the three genies, Zand was their leader and protector. Normally, I was the same with Ali. Tonight, it felt incredible letting someone take charge with me. For him to do whatever he wanted to me—as long as it made Zand forget his pain and helped me ignore losing him in a month.

His huge package dug into my belly. Gods, that was going to fill me. I rubbed against it, coaxing a grunt from him as he buried his face in my neck, sucking, licking, nibbling.

"I'm going to devour you." His breath fanned along my throat, stirring shivers in me.

"I bet you will." I tossed my head back, loving what he was doing to me.

His excitement rubbed me in just the right way, and I rocked against his hard shaft, building my arousal to match his. Gods, I groaned so bad I swear the whole forest could hear me. But I didn't care. He was all mine for now.

Flashing me a smile, his large hand ran along the curve of my back, and down my ass. "You're so beautiful."

"You make me blush with your sweet words. Your touches drive me insane." I stood up, letting him remove my clothes, soft and slow. His hands guide me down to the drawstring of his pants. Soaking in every inch of his body, I took my time sliding off the fabric separating our skin.

"Straddle me." He liked to be in command of the situation. That much was clear. I his willing slave lowered myself over his legs. He cupped one breast and sucked on the other, twirling my tight nipple with his tongue.

I ached for him, shivering for more.

His hand dipped over my sex and rubbed my clit with his thumb. Pulsing with every stroke, I panted and groaned.

Gods. I didn't know how much longer I could take before I burst. Was it possible for me to orgasm from a single caress?

"I can't wait," he growled. "I need you now."

"Take me."

He drove his hard cock into me, his shaft filling me entirely, reaching to the mouth of my womb. A scream pressed the back of my throat. But I didn't let him see my pain and buried my face in his neck. With every plunge into me, it hurt and delighted me in the best possible ways, driving my pulse into a frenzy.

His thirsty hands couldn't get enough of me, rubbing me everywhere, leaving little bolts of red magic sizzling my skin. Was my body electrified from his steady drill into me? Or was it me reacting to his amazing touch? Escalating arousal had my muscles convulsing. He shuddered, and his fingers dug into me.

Gods, his moan was music to my ears.

Right as I was about to peak, he stopped and smiled.

"What are you doing?" I panted.

He stood up, wearing a smirk, and carried me the few steps to the tree, crushing me against the trunk. Our tongues found each other, writhing together. The taste of his kiss was delicious, and I ate him up. Just to tease me, he brushed his hands on the insides of my thighs. His satisfied laugh tickled my ears.

"Please," I begged to the tune of his waving finger.

Whatever he was up to I was up for it, and I raised my pelvis beneath him, showing my eagerness.

Gods. Dahvi was a tease, too. I didn't need two of them driving me crazy!

Zand managed to keep me pressed to the tree as he grabbed two vines dangling from above. He wrapped them over my wrists, tying me up, and stretching my arms above my head. "Hold on, beautiful one."

I did as I was told, totally under his command.

I had to admit, part of this excited the hell out of me, and my pussy throbbing so bad. My insides bursting with anticipation for what came next. But I had to admit that being restricted—having my arms tied—also terrified me. It left me totally at his mercy. What if he hurt me? There was no escape. A shudder rocked through me. Considering my trust issues, I had a hard time letting go and giving up control. But when I looked in his eyes, I only found softness and admiration.

He pulled away, and my legs dropped to the ground. My ankle ached a little, but I pushed aside the pain and ignored it.

His dark eyes drank me up as if he were memorizing every inch of my breasts, my belly, my burning mound. Finally, his gaze lingered on my long legs.

Both my heart and pussy was desperate to take him.

"Don't be scared," he whispered, running his hand down one side of my face. "I won't hurt you."

My heartbeat pounded so hard I thought it might explode.

His hands slid across my waist. He fell to his knees, kissing my inner thighs and then trailing his tongue along my wet and swollen pussy lips. My skin sparked with electricity. With a swift movement, he spread my legs wider, hoisted me into the air, and pressed his face against my tingling folds. Liquid heat gathered between my thighs. He lapped at it, sucking, biting, licking driving me insane.

Back arched, I groaned, writhing, dying in pleasure. I yearned to hold him and run my hands through his hair. A sudden shiver gripped me as he coaxed me to the brink. An orgasm ripped through me and I convulsed, gasping from the waves of desire owning me.

Zand wasn't letting me rest, and he lowered me to his chest level. "Wrap your legs around my waist, master."

Lost in his hypnotic gaze, I followed his lead, allowing my earlier fear to melt away.

He dived into me hard and fast. Each frantic thrust propelled me toward ecstasy. I couldn't control the noises coming from my throat, and he was just as vocal in his pleasure. I swear we must have scared every animal out of the forest. Our bodies fused together, succumbing to the heat between us. Each stroke of my slickness brought me closer to the edge. I rushed toward it with every ounce of my being. His fire sent me rocketing up and over again. Once he finished, he cradled me tight, resting against me, breathing heavy.

I welcomed the break. My body needed to recover from what he'd just done to me. I could still feel his cock stretching me, promising me I'd suffer for this encounter tomorrow, and walking might be painful for a few days. But it would be most delicious and worthwhile, reminding me of out amazing time together.

"I want to do that and so much more," I panted. "Every single day. Three times a day. Once with each of my genies."

Zand smiled and snapped the bindings on my arms. "Your wish is my command."

My wrists hurt a little from the tension I'd placed on them by yanking at them. I rubbed at them, chasing away the burn. "I've never done anything like that before." The words spilled out before I could catch them.

Gods. Heat rose in my cheeks and he stared at me as if demanding an answer. One I delivered him.

"At first I was terrified," I said. "Felt so vulnerable. Worried you would hurt me. But you made me feel so safe. Thank you."

I was so glad I'd let go and trusted him. That he'd been the one to help me do so.

He leaned in and kissed me. For the third time in a matter of a days, my heart caught alight with flames. This time the color was red, representing Zand's magic. Our hearts were bonded just like mine, Dahvi's and Kaza's were.

"Now we are imprinted too." He kissed the tip of my nose.

Curiosity propelled me to search his heart. Zand had felt the call of his heart…his words, not mine…when I plucked him from the lamp. It had changed his pain and set his heart into a confused mess. How he agonized over voiding his deal with the collector. That he was determined not to let her tear him away from his family and I.

I pulled back, startled by the rawness of these revelations. The reminder of what lay ahead for both of us hit me like a blast of sand. It brought up emotions long since buried. Fears of abandonment. Piercing betrayal. Crushing lack to trust anyone. Although I knew the genie's decision aimed it to save his brother, the irrational, frightened little child in me, couldn't accept this. The ache in my chest threatened to tear me in two. Tears pricked my eyes. Sobs burst from my throat.

Zand cupped my face, forcing me to look at him, but my eyes jammed shut. The pain of knowing he was leaving, that our hearts were bound, that I could do nothing about it, was too much to bear.

"Master," his soft whisper caressed my cheek.

"I just need a moment." I slipped out of his grasp and wiped away my tears with the back of my wrist.

My clothes were lying some feet away. I tossed them back on, and strapped my sandals up.

The idea of Zand leaving wasn't the only problem weighing heavy on my mind; I was going to lose my whole genie family. When the time came, and Kaza and Dahvi had fulfilled their duty to me, they, too, would leave me all alone. I couldn't bear the thought. Nor could I cling to a false hope of things working out between the genies and me. One conclusion settled in the pit of my stomach—I wouldn't give in to my developing attraction for the genies any longer. To do so was a recipe for a broken heart. My mother had already done a splendid job of scaring me for life. There was only so much my poor little heart could take.

That was that. My mind was made up then.

"We should head back," I said to Zand. "Administer the sands to Kaza.

While the darkness still provides us cover."

Zand stared at the ground, stiff like a statue. "Yes, Master."

"Call me Azar," I said.

"Yes, Ma—Azar."

His slip up brought a smile to my face.

* * *

BY THE TIME the sun commenced its rise, Dahvi, Zand and I sailed on the magic carpet, over the desert outside Utaara.

The terrain transitioned into paved streets, buildings, temples, palm trees, and shrubs.

Zand tensed, as if sensing danger. "Fire rages in the city."

"What?" I glanced down at Utaara. His words had set off an explosion of nerves in my gut. "How can you tell?"

"My inner flame senses fire," he growled.

The moment he finished speaking, I caught a whiff of something burning. I scanned the city, spotting towering flames dead ahead. The slums. Raging with fire and thick smoke. Whenever a fire got out of control like this, the city rang with warning bells. Not today. Something was seriously wrong. Someone didn't want the warning to sound. The vizier.

Fear crashed inside me.

Ali and Kaza!

CHAPTER 12

*I*ntense heat blasted me as the carpet swooped low, providing us with a better assessment of the situation. The swelter didn't seem to bother the genies. Their affinity for fire probably related to their magical flames.

Below us, people screamed as they ran into the streets, fleeing their burning homes. Children wailed above the roar of fire. Some appeared to have lost their parents and stood fixed to the spot, obviously too terrorized to move. Many fleeing slum residents were apprehended by palace guards who rounded up the crowds and forced them to their knees. Several of the guards brandished swords, threatening those who tried to escape.

The air rushed from my lungs as if I'd been struck by a hammer. What in Utaara was going on? What were the palace guards doing? Were Ali and Kaza still safe in the lamp?

The carpet landed in a back alley a few lanes from all the commotion.

"Where is the thief?" I heard one of the guards shout. "She's committed a treasonous crime against the sultan."

Someone whimpered. "I don't know who you're talking about."

My whole body froze. They were after me. The guards were tearing apart the city, hunting for the genies and me. Under the vizier's orders no doubt. That sick bastard had no heart. Burning down the city to fuel his appetite for power.

Queasiness tumbled inside me.

Ali! Kaza! I had to get to them.

My brain screamed at me to run to my home. But my heart said otherwise. I had to save these people. Their homes were burning because of me. My heart won out, and my feet obeyed, carrying me forward. But I only made it a few yards in the direction of my home before someone caught me by the arm. Strong arms coiled around my waist and lifted me into the air.

"Let me go, Zand." I kicked and hit him, struggling to get loose.

"You're staying with me," he replied, his voice harsh as he moved me aside.

Dahvi's body set alight with pale fire. He raised his hands as if calling something to him. Thick smoke streamed into the lane, leaving a dense haze, from which I could barely see my own hand in front of me. I coughed and covered my nose and mouth with my shawl. Fire weaved through the smog like a flying snake. Tightness strangled my chest. I shielded my eyes from the intense heat.

Zand jammed me against the wall.

"What are you doing?" I banged my fist against his chest. "Let me go or we'll die."

"Cease your protests," he said, grabbing my arms, preventing me from fighting. "I'm protecting you."

To our right I saw the raging fire and smoke pour into Dahvi.

"No!" My breath hiccupped. I wriggled and kicked Zand,

and he squeezed me until my lungs felt as if they might burst. The bond we shared told me the big brute didn't mean me harm. He just wanted me to calm down.

The color of Dahvi's flames intensified as if the fire fueled him. Smoke cleared from the lane. The fire died down until it was nothing but a single flicker in genie's palms.

Gods.

I glanced up finding no more flames crawling on the rooftops of the shacks in the lane.

Exasperated gasps cried out from the slums.

"The fire," yelled someone in the next alley. "It's gone."

"What?" Zand released me and I raced down to the intersection.

Not a lick of fire or smoke anywhere. Scorched buildings were left in its wake. Confused and sooty faces examined the miracle.

I spun around staring at Dahvi. He'd used his magic to absorb the energy from the fire! I was at his side in an instant.

"Thank you." I went to hug him but stopped, unsure if doing so might burn me, but his arms slide around my back and pulled me to him. Luckily he wasn't any steamier than normal.

"Come," said Zand. "Our brothers await."

At the end of the alley, we turned left, then took another right until we reached my home.

I gasped at what was left of it. My hand covered my mouth.

The door was kicked in and resting off its hinges. Someone had smashed the shutters and overturned my furniture.

"Watch her, Brother," said Zand as his shoulders and back twitched, and fire erupted over his body. Like a hulking bear, he thundered into my flat.

"Ali. Kaza," I moaned, scratching at Dahvi's arms.

"Shh," Dahvi whispered, stroking my head with a free hand. "Everything's fine. Zand will get them."

The sick lump in my gut told me otherwise. The guards had found the lamp and had taken my brother and the genie. My thoughts strangled me like vines choking a tree. I was beside myself with grief.

Something crunched underfoot as Zand swept through my shack. Broken pieces of wood rattled. Shards of something—plates, maybe—scraped along the floor. The guards had smashed everything.

Moments later, Zand returned holding his hands behind his back as if hiding something from me.

The lump in my stomach sat like concrete now.

The guards had confiscated the lamp.

Pain cracked down the center of my heart as it split in two.

"What is it?" I shrieked, desperate to know what Zand had found.

Blue smoke fanned around us. In an instant, we were transported elsewhere. Beneath the bridge running over the river that flowed through the city. The sound of water trickled in my ears. Rocks packed the banks to prevent the water from eroding the bridge's foundation. With each passing day, the genie's magic grew stronger.

"What are we doing here?" I asked. "Where is my brother?"

"We are safer here." Zand revealed the contents of his hand.

I gasped at the slumped, lifeless, and blackened corpse of my monkey Karim. His eyes were closed and mouth open as if he'd released his rama—his soul—for the gods to take him to the heavens.

Hands shaking, I clutched my beloved pet to my chest and

clamped my eyes shut. Sobs racked me, and I gasped for air. The monkey had been part of my family. Now he was gone, too. Killed by the vizier's men. This was a warning. More of my loved ones would die if I did not hand over the genies to the vizier.

"No, Karim, no," I moaned, falling to my knees, cuddling my pet.

"I'm so sorry, Azar." Zand's choked voice broke through my bawling.

Dahvi piped in, too. "We won't let the vizier get away with this."

Words were pointless. Nothing either of them said would bring back my pet. And according to genie rules, neither would their magic.

When I opened my eyes again, they were blurred with tears. "Where are our brothers?"

Zand's fists clutched a scroll sealed with wax imprinted with the vizier's symbol.

My throat seized. What was that? An invitation to the palace to visit that sick bastard? A truce? A negotiation? My brother's life in exchange for the genies?

Although Zand offered me the letter, I couldn't move, my whole body paralyzed with fear. Nothing could bring me to read that sick creep's words.

Zand's eyes were pits of regret as he did me the awful honors, tearing off the seal, unraveling the scroll.

My stomach tossed like stormy seas as I stood again.

He cleared his throat and began. "Dearest street rat."

Dahvi squeezed me, as if suspecting I'd fight at the unpleasant title. But I didn't have the strength or will to do so. All my energy focused on where Ali might be and if he was still alive.

"If you want your brother back alive," continued Zand, "bring me the rest of the genies to my chambers in the palace by sunset. Relinquish your claim to the lamp, and I will let your brother go."

Fear tightened my chest until I could barely breathe. My knees weakened beneath me, but Dahvi never let me go.

Ali was all I had left. I could not lose him. A man like the vizier was not going to let Ali and me live once I surrendered the genies. The vizier would slay my brother and me and then dump our bodies in the river, ensuring our silence forever. Was this the fate the gods had chosen for us?

Then what would happen to my city, my home? An evil vizier with three genies by his side...or the power of three genies and his dark flame...was a terrifying prospect. Would he murder the sultan and his family and claim dominion over the kingdom? Kill anyone who did not bow to his leadership? The people of Utaara loved their sultan. Every month, he and his family visited the slums to distribute meals, water, clothes, and blankets to those in need. No one liked the vizier. Around the slums, he'd earned the nickname *yarkosh*, which, roughly translated, meant evil pig. Chaos followed that wicked man, and the people of Utaara would surely revolt. But with the genies by his side, that might lead to death.

Zand crumpled the letter in his fist. Flames licked at its edge, consuming it, until it was nothing more than ashes the wind blew out of his hand.

If I had magic, that was how I would have treated the letter, too. But I didn't.

My shoulders sagged. How was I going to save my brother and the genies? The vizier was right. I was just a mere street rat, good for nothing but stealing.

The weight of my genies' stares landed on me. Were they waiting for a command from me? I couldn't think straight. My mind was a blur of thoughts, clashing against each other like warring swords.

Ali's frightened face flashed in my mind. I pictured him crying as he kneeled at the vizier's feet. Begging for his life. Pleading his innocence. Or frightened inside the lamp as the vizier threatened him.

It felt like a magic bomb had detonated in my chest. That's when the tears came, hard and without mercy.

Dahvi pressed his lips to the side of my head. "Master," he whispered to me. "We will get our brothers back."

Despite the confidence welling in his voice, I didn't agree. The genies hadn't experienced the life-bleeding power of the dark flame the vizier had used to try to kill me. Whatever that thing was, it was powerful. Did my genies even stand a chance against it?

"Ali is our family now, too."

I was touched by Zand's admission. I searched his heart for the meaning of his words. The genie did not just consider me his lover. We were bound, heart and soul. In genie tradition, Ali was regarded as family by extension of me. Zand would fight for Ali's rescue as he would fight for Kaza's freedom.

But before I let either of my genies go magically blast their way into the sultan's palace, I had to tell them about the vizier's dark power. They had to know what we were up against. We had to make a plan.

"What about the vizier's dark magic?" I spluttered. "He tried to kill me with it by draining my life force. I couldn't breathe. My heart stopped beating. It turned my skin grey and cracked. If it wasn't for the lamp's magic, I'd be dead."

Zand's head snapped up. "I will kill him for that."

The promise in his roar frightened me, and I shrank into Dahvi's arms.

"But you can't kill anyone," I reminded him.

Zand's shoulders and back curled forward. "There is always a way."

Flames burst to life on his mane of dark hair. Dahvi's magic carpet appeared mid-air, and Zand jumped onto it.

"Where are you going?" I asked.

I wrestled Dahvi, and finally, he released me.

"To scout out the palace." Zand's voice told me he was not going to be convinced to do otherwise.

"You can't leave us." I seized his arm. "What if they catch you, too?"

I wanted to tell him I couldn't lose him, too, but the words jammed in my throat. Along with my heart.

But Zand understood. I read it in his eyes. Felt him search my heart.

"I must," he said.

He did not meet my eye as he yanked his arm from me. I knew if he did, his heart would tell him to stay by my side, and he wouldn't be able to argue against it. The pinch in his chest told me the pain it cost him to leave me and his brother. I felt it, too, deep in my breast.

Wind blasted me back into Dahvi's arms as Zand's carpet shot into the air, above the bridge, and over a row of mud-brick buildings.

My heart was heavy at him leaving. Gone without even giving me a kiss. At least Kaza would have blown me one or given me a wink.

Cradling Karim, I regained my balance, staring up after my lover. Sunlight seared my eyes as I watched him disappear from sight. Part of me hoped he would return straight away, realizing his mistake. But after a minute or so, I knew that wasn't going to happen.

In the back of my mind, I dreaded Zand's return and what news he'd bring. That future moment marked my fate. Life or death. I was not running away with Dahvi and leaving Ali, Kaza, or Zand in the hands of the vizier.

I bent down and placed Karim on the banks. Rocks

clunked as I shifted them, making way for his burial hole. Dirt built under my fingernails as I scratched a grave deep enough to bury my sweet monkey. Eyes burning with tears, I placed his lifeless body in the hole and filled it back up. Atop this, I replaced the stones, leaving three on top to signal his grave. I didn't have anything to leave him as a tribute.

A beautiful sunflower materialized in my hand.

I glanced over at Dahvi and smiled my thanks. Between two rocks, I stuck the flower. It wasn't enough, but it was all I had to give beside my sweet monkey and thanks for many wonderful years.

The pain in my chest tripled, and I slumped in Dahvi's arms again. Emotions welled up in my chest like a blocked pipe ready to burst. Something shifted, and they exploded in a torrent of tears, anger, hurt, and devastation. My heart ached to have Karim, Ali, and my two genies back. A darkness pressed against the back of my mind. A great fear, building like a bubbling, dark mass, ready to consume me if they were harmed, and I lost them, too.

Dahvi crushed me to him. His lips buried in my hair.

I clutched him for dear life. "Please, don't leave me."

"Never," he whispered. "I am yours forever."

Was he just saying that because as a genie he belonged to me?

He lifted my chin so our eyes met. "My heart is yours."

For the first time in my life, the ice surrounding my heart melted. After losing my mother, and my first boyfriend, I had convinced myself I wasn't worthy of love and happiness. Here I was, finding the romance I craved, and with three genies! That filled me with hope that I might get the happily ever after I yearned for.

One hand cupped the back of my neck. Dahvi's lips pressed mine, soft and sweet and deliciously warm. A radiating heat spread from my mouth to the tips of my toes. I welcomed it. I needed it. To take away my fears and heart-break. Hunger for Dahvi consumed me, and I sucked his lower lip, bringing on his soft moan. He ran his hands through my hair. His tongue explored mine, twisting, suck-ing. All of it left me breathless and insatiable.

Dahvi's hands explored every inch of me. My arms, sides, and legs buzzed from his touch. I coiled my arms around his neck, wanting to forget everything, even if it was just for a minute. After all, this might be my last day in Haven. I moaned from the sweet trail of sweet kisses he left along my neck.

Unexpectedly, the genie pulled away. "Sit, Azar." It was weird hearing him call me by my name. I let him guide me to a patch of greenery by the river. "You need to rest before we go to the palace."

Right now, I just wanted to be held. To not think about anything. But that wouldn't solve anything, would it? I needed some time to process everything that had happened and build a plan of attack. There I sat, watching the flowing water, the blue genie's hand in mine.

I didn't want to ask, but I had to. "What will we do if the vizier kills Kaza and my brother?"

"Don't think about that, Azar."

Dahvi's optimism annoyed me, and I scowled. "But we have to be prepared."

Dahvi issued a long sigh. "Under djinn law, if one of our own is slain by another, we may honor our fallen, and avenge their death."

His answer took me by surprise. That someone as gentle as him had said such a thing. That he'd even considered a law that countenanced the slaying of another.

Any idiot would know I'd do anything for my brother. Anything. But exchanging the genies for his life equaled their deaths. With the dark flame, the vizier could siphon their power and kill them. Even though I was a thief, I still lived by a code, and murder was not one I subscribed to. Such was my dilemma. My heart was linked to all of them. There was no way in hell I'd let the vizier take anyone else from me.

The name Azar translated to Gods' flame. I'd be damned if I'd let the vizier destroy everything I loved. I swore I would burn him to the ground for what he had done. I kept repeating the promise in my head. A promise I would deliver personally.

CHAPTER 13

*L*ost in my thoughts, I didn't notice Zand return until the whoosh of his carpet blasted my hair all over my face.

Elated to see him again, I jumped up to greet him with a long hug. One I didn't want to ever end, but knew it must—we had to save our brothers.

"What did you find?" My words came out fast. "Where are our brothers?"

Zand's forehead pinched. "They were both removed from the lamp and are being held in the vizier's tower."

Tension in my stomach eased a little, knowing my brother was not being kept prisoner in those filthy dungeons where his illness might have deteriorated.

"Your brother is chained to the floor." Zand ground his teeth as if he was preparing to smash something. "The guards have laid hands on him."

"What?" I grabbed a rock and heaved it at one of the bridge's columns, chipping off some concrete.

Fire boiled in my chest. The fire of life and death. Together, my genies and I would save everyone we loved, destroy the vizier, and live out our days by the ocean. With every passing second, my mind raged with wildfire. I had to leave and get my brother and Kaza back before it was too late. Before I could catch up with my feet, they had carried me halfway up the riverbank.

Zand and Dahvi shouted behind me, their words white noise barely registering above the crackling and spitting of the blaze set off in me.

A hand caught my arm and yanked me back. It took a few seconds before it dawned on me that Zand had stopped me. Dahvi stood closely behind him, his body rigid.

"I'm going to make that wretch, the vizier, pay." Venom coated my words. It shocked me at the same time. I hadn't spoken of anyone like this since I cracked a chair over the orphanage director's head.

"Azar, we can't rush in there." The tone in Zand's voice told me that would not be wise.

"The vizier has laid traps everywhere," he added.

I pressed my hands to my hips. "I'm a thief, remember? I can get in anywhere."

"These traps are invisible to human eyes," he replied. "Existing on higher planes. Like where my brothers and I are from."

A terrible dread scratched at my gut. How the hell did the vizier know how to do that? Something told me I wasn't going to like the answer.

The tightness in Zand's mouth told me he didn't like the answer either. "The vizier is a powerful sorcerer, versed in the arts of dark magic."

Haunting memories of my first meeting with the vizier sprang to mind. His eyes had turned black, and I'd felt a sickening dread as my life force had bled into his dark flames. Dear gods, I'd almost met my end.

I waved my hands around as I paced. "You're both genies. Can't you protect us against the vizier's dark magic?"

"To an extent," said Zand. "We use light magic for the purpose of good, only. It, like dark magic, has its limits. But for the right price, let's say a sacrifice, dark magic can be enhanced…"

I didn't like the way his words trailed off and braced myself for a dump of bad news. A sacrifice? Like my brother's or Kaza's life? A pit opened up in my stomach.

"Let's just say," said Dahvi, finishing for his brother, "we're not sure how powerful this dark flame is. We've heard rumors about how it corrupted our Mother Queen. When she used it to siphon energy from the Marid djinn, granting her more power, the darkness overwhelmed and killed her."

What a horrible story, but secretly, I hoped the same fate befell the vizier. Would serve him right for playing with dark things he shouldn't mess with.

"Well," I said, lifting my arms high out of frustration. "What's the plan?"

"Black magic is most powerful at the peak of the night," explained Zand. "As the sun sets, his power will grow stronger. We must get him at his weakest. Trap and bind him."

I glanced up at the golden orb, sitting at the midday position in the sky. Light magic at its strongest. With two genies by my side, I had no doubt we could defeat the scumbag vizier and get Ali and Kaza back.

"Can we somehow trap the vizier in the lamp?" I asked.

Both Zand and Dahvi nodded.

"To get the lamp, we will need to sneak in," said Zand.

Hah! Finally, my skills would come in handy. *Thank the gods.* I'd felt so useless without any magic to contribute.

"Okay," I said. "I know a few ways in."

"No." Zand grabbed my hand and ran his thumb over it.

Fire scorched through me, leaving me breathless and wishing he'd never let me go.

His next words brought me crashing back to reality. "During my surveillance of the palace, I found four tunnels, one leading to each tower of the palace."

I'd never heard a whisper about any tunnels. Nor had I found any evidence of them in all my sneaking around. I'd been everywhere in Utaara, and there was no place I couldn't find a way into. I searched Zand's heart, and images flashed in my mind of even more tunnels, all of them connecting to different realms within Haven.

Perfect. Once we defeated the vizier, we had an escape route to the ideal little life I envisioned by the sea. If that option didn't work out, we could find a new home in either The Cove or near Scarlet in Terra.

"Where do we find these tunnels?" I asked, bursting with excitement to retrieve Ali and Kaza and to start our new life.

"I tracked an entrance back to a wall a few blocks to the north," said Zand. "But there is a door sealed by magic."

Of course, there was. The vizier had cast it himself.

Zand touched the band on his wrist. "No. This is the work of a djinn."

Recollections flew back to me of the city circle tower, which people said was haunted by a djinn. They left tributes there in hopes the djinn might grant their wish. And it did sometimes. How the djinn managed to do so while trapped, I didn't know...the entire concept didn't seem to make sense. Then again, neither did genie magic or dark sorcerer power.

"A djinn is more powerful than a genie," Zand said. "With our limited magic, we might not be able break its spell."

A drowning sensation captured my gut.

Something poked me in the back, and I twirled to find Dahvi's magical carpet waving a tassel at me to get onboard.

As always, Dahvi lifted me onto it, and Zand leaped on beside us.

Did I mention I loved having genies by my side? Zand for protection. Dahvi to comfort me. Kaza to make me laugh. I set my mind to the fact that soon we'd be reunited as a family.

Normally, I was the planning type, laying out every part of my mission in advance. Entry and exit points. Spare tools for unforeseen circumstances. Various "Plan Bs" in reserve in case of emergencies. But today, I was going in completely unprepared and out of my depth, to fight against an evil sorcerer wielding dark magic. A sudden coldness tightened around my entire body. What was I getting myself into?

At the djinn wall in the center of the city, rock scraped as Zand's magic shifted a loose block about the size of a tiger, leaving a space wide enough for Dahvi and I to hunch down and enter. Stale air, probably hundreds of years old, blasted us, and I coughed, pulling my shirt over my nose.

"Gods, I can hardly breathe in here," I said.

"Shall I make it smell like roses?" Dahvi adopted the smartass tone I'd expect from Kaza.

Either Dahvi missed his brother, or he was trying to lighten the mood. Gods knew, I needed something to take my mind off this rescue. For the last hour, a vice had clamped down on my heart, one I knew wouldn't let go until my brother and the genie were safe and sound, and we were a thousand miles from here. But humor always did the trick when it came to making me a little less stressed.

I tickled his armpit for being cheeky, and he gave me a quick kiss.

Zand closed the stone block behind us, releasing a puff of dust that stuck to my hair and eyes. I blinked a few times to dislodge the dirt and rubbed the rest away.

I groped around in the pitch black that had swallowed us. "A little light, please."

"We must conserve as much magic as possible," warned Zand.

Fire snapped to life, crackling and writhing on his palms. Its illumination stretched about twenty feet in either direction, revealing the same view on both ends. Large bricks, stained with red iron marks from water dripping down the sides. Tree roots crawled along the wall, seeking the water, ending where they found it. Spiders hunched in their webs, which clung to the corners. Gods only knew where they got their food when there wasn't another bug in sight.

The chill clinging to the air raked along my skin, and I rubbed my arms for warmth. Arachnids and darkness didn't bother me. What turned my bowels to water was the thought of the evil awaiting us in the palace.

Dahvi ran his palm flames along my upper arm, and an invigorating warmth filled me, chasing away my fears. Dahvi —my strength, my rock. I leaned into him so our arms just touched. Fire sizzled between us. I needed his calming energy right now. The possibility of losing my brother was turning me into a crazy mess, and only Dahvi kept me sane.

"Thanks," I said, looking up at him through my lashes.

"Anything for you," said Dahvi, flashing his gorgeous smile.

Awww. I loved how adorable he was. Out of all my genies, he was the most considerate and the sweetest. I didn't know what I would have done without him by my side.

"Enough of that, Brother," said Zand, kicking Dahvi's behind playfully and pushing him forward.

I loved this fresh, new side to Zand. His stiff broodiness got a bit boring.

I laughed and smacked him on the ass. "Don't get jealous."

Zand offered me an urgent kiss before moving on. "I'm not. I just don't want him getting all the attention."

I touched my lips, which were tingling from the impact of both their kisses, and smiled. Gods, they were sexy. Once my brother was safe and the vizier dead, I fantasized about bringing each of them back here for some alone time. Separately, of course. I imagined each of them, fucking me all day until my pussy stung from too much sex. I pictured myself screaming as loudly as I wanted, with no one to hear me. Heat pooled between my thighs, but I pushed those thoughts aside to concentrate on Ali and Kaza's rescue.

Our footsteps crunched on the ground as we made our way deeper into the tunnels. Silence suffocated us, as if the genies had descended into dark thoughts of their own. Based on the stiffness in Zand's expression, I assumed he'd prepared an attack of his own on the vizier. The deep lines in Dahvi's forehead told me he worried for his brother's safety.

More than anything, I wished someone would say something because my mind, too, kept drifting to endless possibilities that could go wrong. I blamed it on us not having a backup plan in case of an emergency. Winging it was at odds with the planner in me.

"So, what are we going to do with the vizier?" I broke the silence as I stepped over a tree root jutting out of the ground. "Kill him? Imprison him in a land far away? Stuff him in the lamp?"

"I vote for the first option," said Dahvi. The lightheartedness he'd shown earlier had all but disappeared.

"Careful, Brother," warned Zand. "You know the rules."

Oh, Zand... Such a stickler for genie law. We'd only reserved that plan if the vizier killed anyone.

An unexpected tremor rocked the passage, and we all crashed into the wall. The shuddering vibrated all the way up my legs. A deep groan echoed down the tunnel beneath the palace. It sounded like the whole place was about to collapse or something. It was almost as if the vizier had ears in the tunnel, heard our plan, and decided to attack first, to kill us before we could reach him.

A lump sprang up in my throat. I spun around, squinting into the darkness at the edge of Dahvi's flame.

"What was that?" I asked.

Zand tilted his head, as if listening. "The djinn who sealed the tunnels is here."

I glanced at Dahvi, but he, too, was focused, as if a voice from another world called to him.

"The vizier is a sorcerer of old," Zand repeated, as if passing on the story. "His dark magic trapped her in the city's walls for three hundred years."

That bastard! How many other creatures had he abused for the sake of accumulating his power? My stomach prickled with remorse for the poor djinn. I couldn't imagine being bound to the city for several lifetimes.

Dahvi spoke up. "Our sister requests our help in getting free."

Geez. The quaking sure was a funny way of asking for help.

Fissures snaked across the ground as another quake rumbled. This one was much stronger, and I almost lost my balance.

Zand grabbed me protectively, pulling me up against him, steadying me.

My fingers dug into his waist.

"She doesn't agree with us taking a human as a mate," advised Zand.

My chest thrummed at the mention of the word mate, pumping a delicious, electric charge through me. Until now, I'd never been anyone's mate. Hadn't been looking, to be honest. Beyond my own basic needs, my brother's health and survival was my first priority. Everything had changed the second I had met the genies. Having three mates made me the luckiest girl in Haven.

I pushed aside those thoughts for the moment. For now, I just wanted to focus on one thing at a time. Prime objective number one: save my brother and Kaza, and in the process, don't gain any new enemies, like a cranky djinn.

"Brother, look." Dahvi pointed to the tree roots on the wall.

A black mass crawled over them, burning the fibers and turning them to ash. Dark veins stretched through the bricks. Sand on the ground blackened as if burned.

Suddenly, a sickening nausea gripped me, and I didn't feel so confident in our odds. "The dark flame."

The quaking and groaning ended at the mention of those words.

Like we needed any more magic to contend with. Wasn't the vizier, the dark flame, and a severely pissed-off djinn enough to deal with?

"Watch your step," said Zand, taking careful steps, as if avoiding booby traps.

Nerves tense, gut clenched, I followed close behind him in case I needed a magical get-away from my buried prison beneath the streets of Utaara.

Gods knew how much time passed before we reached a sealed door with strange markings carved into it. I sure hoped Zand could do his magical shifting trick; otherwise, we might have to return the way we'd come and sneak in the old-fashioned way. My way.

Pushing past Zand, I let my fingers trace the foreign symbols. The marks scorched with magical fire and spat embers.

Zand ran his finger along a circle carved in the stone, exposing more writing, which he read out loud. "Here rests the mighty djinn Wanessa. Punished for refusing to do the vizier's bidding. Only when she performs the spell she was summoned for, or the vizier leaves this Earthly plane, will she be released."

Well. That was easily solved, then, wasn't it? We were going to slay the vizier and free this djinn.

"Our poor sister."

The forlorn tone in Dahvi's voice made my heart ache.

Both genies pressed their foreheads to the door as if it were some sort of djinn ritual.

When Zand straightened, he placed a hand in the circle at the center of the door. Fiery shapes shifted across its surface. Fireworks flashed outward like party sparklers. Rock cracked and groaned as it inched open. Sand poured off the top of the door. The noise slammed down the corridor.

Uneasiness tumbled inside me. I half expected to encounter something nasty on the door's other side. Guards with swords raised, ready to slice me to bits. A three-headed dragon or something, waiting to roast us to a crisp. The vizier with a ball of dark flame to turn us to ash. But none of that presented itself. Only a dusty stairwell, lit by blazing torches. Something about the glowing stairway didn't feel right. As if someone had expected our arrival via this route. I mean, who would light torches in a stairway leading to tunnels sealed by magic doors? It almost felt as if the vizier had anticipated this move.

CHAPTER 14

A sudden wind picked up in the tunnel, tossing my hair over my shoulders. Sand swirled on the ground, in small circles at first, then widening and lifting into the air, until it was a miniature whirlwind.

My stomach locked tight as things got even crazier.

The building tornado pounded us with dirt, cobwebs, water droplets, and dust. I lost sight of my genies through the haze tearing around us. Fear clutched at my throat as I groped blindly for them, grazing one of their arms. Wind ripped at my clothes, dragging me away, and my feet scraped along the ground.

"Azar," shouted Zand.

"Where are you?" I yelled back.

Strong hands grabbed my waist, steadying me.

Zand.

But even his great strength wasn't enough to keep us rooted. Gale-force winds tossed us aside, and we crashed into a wall, pinned there by the wind's pressure.

At that instant, my life flashed before my eyes. Death snaring my genies and me in the tunnel. Ali and Kaza, perishing at the hands of the vizier or their infections. My heart shrank at the thought.

The debris hitting us eased off, allowing me to glance up.

A feminine shape made of sand began to form inside the whirlwind—first her legs, then her torso, her arms, her shoulders, and her head. With a loud snap, the dirt transformed into skin and bone. In an instant, the squall died down, but my ears still rang from all the noise.

A djinn stood before us…more precisely, a Shaitan like Kaza, judging by her golden crop top and rippling, silk pants. Talk about a looker. Perfect golden skin without any blemishes. Hair, whisked up in a tight ponytail and not a single lock out of place. She stood tall, with plenty of cleavage on display, making my small chest feel inadequate by comparison. Large, round eyes, haunted by years of captivity within the city's wall, watched us.

Why had my genies chosen me as their mate over someone as goddess-like as her? Or the several thousand other stunners back in djinn land?

Dahvi scraped to his feet from the wall opposite us.

Something about her cold expression didn't sit right in my belly. I scrambled over to yank him back down, but he moved out of my reach.

Zand remained by my side like a good guard dog. He grabbed me tight, as if ready to spin me out of harm's way in a second. Still, his protective presence didn't settle the uneasy feeling in my guts.

"Sister," Dahvi cried, rushing to give the djinn a hug.

Dark lightning charged on the onyx wristbands she wore —symbols of her imprisonment to the vizier. She raised a palm covered in henna tattoos stretching all the way up her arm. But that didn't stop the big, cuddly genie. At his embrace, she stiffened, and her expression hardened. Her yellow irises flashed with magic. Another blustery wind whisked Dahvi away, tossing him at the wall, and he thudded onto the ground beside us.

"Dahvi!" Instinctively, I jerked free of Zand to go to my blue genie.

A force smacked me against the bricks. Pain splinted up my spine and through my skull. For a few moments, I couldn't see past the black dots blurring my vision. When my eyes refocused, I found the same invisible hand holding Zand, too.

"Sorry, Brothers," said the djinn, her voice icy and her wristbands spitting dark bolts of magic. "But the vizier gave me a choice. My freedom or yours."

Shock struck me like lightning. That bitch. She was betraying her kind. The selfish part of me understood the Shaitan's need for survival. But the compassionate side did not.

Several balls of lava pelted the Shaitan. She screamed, clutching her arm, and stumbled backward.

The djinn's magic hold on me released.

Zand's stance declared war, legs and arms spread wide. He was ready to get the djinn if she made another move.

An assault of wind battered us, slamming me to the ground. Being the easy target didn't sit well with me. I wasn't going to get ten meters down the hall without being beaten to death by the Shaitan's air magic.

The genies held their ground, lifting their arms to shield their eyes.

A tight ball of panic looped in my chest. I had to face facts; we were in deep trouble. My genies still weren't at full capacity, and they'd be facing off with a more powerful being that could kick their asses. But if they couldn't get past her, we stood no chance of saving Ali and Kaza.

"Brother," said Zand, handing Dahvi the glass containing the magical sands. "Give this to Kaza. I'll handle this."

Dahvi accepted the cure with a nod.

"What?" I backed away, unable to handle the heat Zand gave off. "No!"

Deep in my soul, I knew I couldn't stop him. He'd die fighting to save me. Each of his steps forward told me that was his plan.

"We have no quarrel with you, Sister," warned Zand. "Join us, and we will help you get free."

"You can't defeat the vizier," snarled the Shaitan, black streaks of magic circling her. "He keeps me trapped here with his dark magic."

Suddenly our odds of success felt incredibly small. Having to fight a djinn then the vizier.

Dahvi flung me behind him.

A vortex spun around the Shaitan as she beat at Zand with all her might. He struggled against the bluster, inching forward slowly. Several fireballs exploded off him and pounded her. The force field of wind swirling around her deflected the attack, tossing them onto the bricks, which melted beneath the fiery assault.

I peeked around Dahvi, digging my nails into his arms. Watching the two fight, I felt utterly powerless. With every fiber of my being, I longed to tear that bitch's head off for siding with the vizier. For daring to threaten my genies and me. But that was never going to happen in a million years.

Zand jabbed a glowing arm through the Shaitan's winds, grabbing her by the neck and choking her. She kicked at him, punching him with one hand as she waved the other, as if she was calling to someone or something. Black tendrils reached out and struck the wall. Blocks grazed across each other as they shifted. Two flung through the air.

Dahvi pushed me to the ground. The bricks smashed on the wall above us and thumped onto the ground next to us.

"Very well." Zand crushed the Shaitan against the wall. "You made your choice, Sister."

She scratched at his arm, assaulting him with magic, dulling and shrinking his red flames. Using what little magic he had recuperated weakened his inner flame. How much longer could he hold off the Shaitan?

Dahvi scooped me into his arms. "Come. Let us get our brothers."

"We can't leave him—"

Dahvi silenced my protests by tossing out a blast of magic, and it trailed along the walls. The tree roots responded, growing in size and crawling along the stone. They seized the Shaitan, tying her to the wall.

Dahvi carried me into the stairwell. "Zand has faced worse. She's a Shaitan. They're not as powerful as Ifrit."

"Yes, but he's a genie and not at full power," I contended.

"Neither is she," replied Dahvi, carrying us down a long hall. "Dark magic binds her power to the city. She cannot utilize it all until she's released."

This news comforted me somewhat. At least the Shaitan and Zand were on somewhat of an even playing field.

Within a few moments, we'd reached the vizier's tower, where Dahvi paused at the bottom of the staircase. For a moment, we stared deep into each other's eyes. Waves of Marid magic floated around his pupils. Love for me radiated deep within his soul. It flowed from me, too. We hugged for a long moment before he pulled away.

"Ready?" he asked, lowering me to the marble staircase.

"Ready," I said with a forceful nod, even though my gut told me otherwise.

What we encountered in the vizier's tower at the top was not what I had expected. I imagined shadow central, red eyes in the darkness, putrid, rotting garbage, and the smell of decay. To my surprise, tall arches and columns allowed plenty of light to filter through. Colored silks puffed from the breezes straying in from the balcony. Incense sticks burned, spreading the scent of frankincense through the tower. Candles flickered in the stained-glass lamps dangling from the ceiling. Geometric-patterned tiles decorated the floors and walls. Gold inlaid practically every item of furniture, showing no expense had been spared.

Hated to say it, but I had to admit the vizier's taste in furnishings were pretty classy...unlike the man himself.

We continued into the next room, where Dahvi stopped dead.

Chains bound Kaza to the floor. Golden streams of magic teamed off him and into the dark flame flickering on a marble stand. Bits of his gray, cracked skin flaked off. His torso sagged over his bent legs.

My pulse streamed. Where was Ali? Did the vizier have him chained somewhere else? Was he already dead? The last thought ground my insides to pieces.

Dahvi and I were at Kaza's side in a flash.

"Brother!" Dahvi clutched Kaza's face and lifted it. Dahvi's skin darkened from the effect of the dark flame.

The yellow gave me a weak wink. "There's my desert queen," he croaked.

"Oh, my love." I stroked his face, and the same darkness touched me. "Are you all right? Where is Ali?"

"Never been better." Kaza feigned a smile, but behind his expression I sensed his torture. "That old sack of bones has our little brother."

I smiled. Knowing Kaza considered Ali a part of his family made me feel good. Using our bond, I searched inside Kaza, sensing his declining heartbeat. By the looks of it, he didn't have long before his life force gave out completely. The ache in my chest threatened to split me in two. We had to get him out of here, but how? Messing with the dark flame would mean certain suicide, and I didn't know any magic to free him.

"Which one of you devils farted in the lamp?" asked Kaza.

Gods. Always a joker. But this wasn't the time or place to goof around.

"Whoever it was," warned Kaza, "there's a prank coming your way."

I imagined Kaza setting up some elaborate practical joke —but only if we survived.

Dahvi laughed. "Wouldn't have it any other way, Brother."

"Hurry up and kill that sack of bones, would you?" said Kaza.

My fingers itched for it. For my freedom. For the genies' freedom. For my brother's life. For my new family.

"Welcome." The eerie, familiar voice came from a darkened hallway. "I wasn't expecting you so early."

The vizier!

All over my body pinched as if ants nipped at me. My suspicions that he'd been expecting us were horribly confirmed.

The creep slid out of the shadows, clutching my brother's shoulder with his bony fingers. Chains on Ali's wrists and ankles clinked as he shuffled forward. Bruises marked his cheeks and arms and even his chest above the line of his cotton shirt. Lines streaked his dirty face, no doubt caused by the tears he'd cried.

I didn't need genie magic to stir my inner fire. God's fire blazed all throughout my body.

"Hand over my brother," I said, refusing to let this creep say too much when his voice grated on my every nerve.

A long laugh bellowed from the vizier, and he steepled his fingers. "My dear, street rat. You are not in a position to negotiate."

I still have two genies, buddy. Well...one at the moment.

"Ali," I said, struggling to remain calm for his sake. "I'll get you out of here, okay?"

My brother whimpered as the vizier rolled his wrist and hand.

Dahvi stormed forward. Dark characters representing some foreign language glowed on the marble he stepped on. Black flames sprung out of the floor. A grey cone of energy rose from the floor surrounding him. He smacked into it and stumbled backward, holding his nose.

The vizier wore a smile like a vulture about to dine on a camel. "I'm afraid, dear street rat, that all your bargaining chips are now in my possession."

Dahvi smashed his fist against the barrier trapping him. Blue ripples radiated outward from the gloom. The panic claiming his face cut at my insides.

"No." I put my hands where Dahvi's were, and electricity zapped me, and I stepped back.

Two genies out of action didn't leave me much to work with. I could only pray to the gods that Zand came out of his battle alive and with some juice left to take on the vizier.

Another laugh erupted from the evil man. He enjoyed playing with people. The cat hunting the mice. This bastard was sick.

My heart screamed at me to crack him on the nose. My mind said otherwise. The creep had untold dark magic. That left me with nothing to fight with. What was I going to do? When Zand showed up, was he going to walk into another trap, too? Then what? We'd really be stuffed.

The vizier glanced over my shoulder and clapped his hands as if he was delighted with something.

Then I heard it. Someone groaning. Something being dragged along the floor.

My stomach plummeted to my toes. Every muscle tensed as I turned.

The Shaitan entered the room, dragging Zand by one wrist. Bruises marked his entire body, and blood wept from several wounds. What had she done to him? How had she defeated him? Last time I'd seen him, he had taken some blows, but overall, he'd seemed to have the upper hand.

I pressed my open palm against my stomach. "Zand," I whimpered. Stinging tears pricked my eyes, and my hands flew to my mouth. No. Not Zand. My protector. My last hope, trickling down the drain.

Defeat flashed in his eyes as his gaze met mine. Our connection told me he was badly wounded both physically and magically.

I wanted to scream.

The Shaitan bitch dropped Zand, and his torso thumped onto the ground. She smiled at me and kicked him, sending him sliding across the floor. He stopped right next to Dahvi. The same foreign writing activated on the marble. Dark flames circled Zand and a cone of magic circled him, too.

My blood rushed through my veins like a shooting star. She'd picked the wrong side. I didn't know how, but I would kill her.

The vizier collected the dark fire in his palm. "Very good, my dear djinn," he said, running his hands across the flames, as if stroking a pet.

It sent a sickening chill through me that filled me with dread. I felt the call of its darkness, like I had the last time we'd met.

"Now grant my freedom, sorcerer," said the Shaitan.

"Once the genies' powers are mine, I shall set you free."

CHAPTER 15

I backed away, tripping over the edge of the rug. My backside hit the floor.

The vizier let out a cruel laugh that bounced off the wall. "There's no one to save you now, street rat." The edge of malice in his voice promised me a painful death.

I shrank away from him, unsure how to save my brother and genies and get the hell out of there. By the look of it, we were well and truly screwed. Ali and I would meet our ends, our bodies tossed into the river.

I glanced at my genies. Dahvi's gaze was glued to Kaza.

Zand said something, but I couldn't make out the words. Frustrated, he yelled and pointed at something to my right.

I scanned around the room for what he meant. Was he trying to point out a weapon to fight the vizier? Sure, I cold bash him over the head with a hookah pipe, but that wouldn't kill him. Maybe choke him with some silks. Burn his eyes out with some incense?

"Now that everyone is assembled, I have no need for this little flea anymore." The vizier pushed my brother to the floor.

"Ali." I crawled on hands and knees across to him.

"What do you want me to do with them?" the Shaitan asked.

Zand's fingers twitched, as if he was pointing at something.

My gaze followed his line of direction, my gaze landing on a white column with gold-leaf embellishment at the top. What was so special about that?

"Kill them," replied the vizier. "Throw their bodies to the sharks."

Anger pulsed within me, hungry for the destruction of both of them.

Zand jabbed with more fury and mouthed the words "dark flame." What was he trying to tell me?

I tried to connect to his heart, but there was only darkness. *Damn it.*

My gaze flew to Dahvi, hoping he understood and could help me out. He, too, pointed at the column.

What was so special about it?

Think. Think. What was my genies' plan? Smash the dark flame into the column? Cause a chain reaction and blow up the palace? But what about everyone else who lived within the walls? My mind was such a blur.

The Shaitan gravitated in our direction. She seized my brother by the throat and lifted him into the air. Ali's dangling legs kicked as he tried to break free.

Fear clawed across my body.

"Ali, no!" I launched to my feet.

My fingernails dug into my palm as I curled my fist. Filled with the fierceness of a mother bear protecting her cubs, I cracked her right in the nose. Blood poured out her nostrils, and she stumbled backward.

Huh! Djinn bled, too.

My brother slumped to the ground.

For laying a finger on him, I kicked her in the gut.

Residue from Zand's fight clung to her. I sensed it. She was burned, wounded, and weakened from their fight. It wasn't going to take much to push her over the edge.

I'd been in many scrapes as a youngster. In the orphanage. On the streets against older and bigger kids. I could handle myself in a fight. As long as the Shaitan didn't unleash her power on me, we were on an even playing field.

"Get up, you fool," shouted the vizier.

I'd deal with him next.

While the Shaitan was bleeding and distracted, I made my move. The heel of my foot laid waste to her consciousness. Her head smacked against the marble. Out cold, she'd no longer been a problem.

Hah! I'd just beaten a djinn without any magic. This gave me confidence I could take on the vizier. But I may have to weaken him first.

Dahvi cheered me on from inside his prison.

Zand flashed me a proud smile and pointed to the column again.

What was up with that?

A wave of the vizier's hand made the dark fire grow. Darkness replaced the white in his eyes. His skin took on a gray pallor as if the dark magic absorbed his life force. But I knew that was a fool's hope. The evil power was only fueling him with shadow, rage, and vengeance.

A blast of his gloomy magic struck me, lowering me to my knees. The evil power sank its claws into me. My life force bled from me as it had the last time, feeding the dark magic. Energy stripped out of my muscles. My heartbeat slowed. Breaths were stolen from my lungs, and I gasped, clawing at my throat.

Eyes closed, the vizier seemed drunk on the power flowing into him.

My gaze swung around the room. There was no Karim to save me now. The guards had seen to that by setting my house ablaze.

Ali crawled closer me to from my right.

Kaza groaned to my left.

The genies were trapped in front of me. Both of them trained their finger at the column.

Against the blood draining away and the energy being zapped from it, my mind scrambled to make sense of the genies' meaning. What did they want me to do?

Then I saw them. The trails of black dots on the floor, leading to their jails.

Something Zand had said before we entered the tunnels clicked in my mind. On his scout of the palace, he'd seen traps buried beneath the floor. But how did they work? What did the column have to do with it?

By this point, Ali had reached me. "No, Azar, no."

When he touched me, the darkness crawled along his skin, and he sucked in a breath. I was powerless to push him away.

"Break the traps," he whispered in my ear.

With what? I glanced again at the column, and the answer finally hit me. *Gods.* I was so stupid. Make the post fall. How the heck was I going to achieve that? I couldn't just punch the thing and make it topple. But if I could hit it hard enough, then it might fall.

I glanced at Zand.

His eyes begged for me to stay alive.

The fog in my mind cleared a little. Finally, I understood his message. Get the vizier to strike the column with his magic. Maybe, in the process, I'd weaken him, too, like he'd done to Zand. Then, once my genies were free of their traps, they could burn him to a crisp.

When I glanced up, I caught sight of Ali hobbling straight for the vizier.

Shish kebab. What was he doing? I couldn't find my voice. It was jammed way down in my throat thanks to the dark magic bleeding me.

I wished Ali could kick the evil vizier in the balls, but that wasn't happening with my brother's chained feet. Instead, Ali lifted his hands and clunked the end of his wrist chains on the vizier's forehead. Just like Karim had done. Ali would have made the monkey so proud!

The blow shook the vizier from his stupor.

All claim on my life from the dark flame faltered. Energy seeped back into me. My chest pumped air through my body. Blood crashed through my veins.

The vizier batted away my brother with a powerful blast.

"No!" Power returned to my limbs in a torrent of fury. I stumbled to my feet. Woozy and unsteady, I stomped forward.

In my mind, I apologized for not going straight to Ali, but any deviation from the plan might end us all.

The vizier's glare cut into me. He aimed a finger me.

But with each step, my energy returned.

I ducked as another of the vizier's detonations exploded above me. I'd always been fast—other than the one time the vizier's guard had gotten me. I did have an injured foot. Today, history was not going to repeat. I dived another discharge and rolled along the floor.

More bombs went off. For a dark sorcerer, the vizier was a pretty awful shot. But I didn't begrudge him that because it kept me alive longer.

Just a few more yards.

Up on my feet, I grabbed anything small. Candleholders sailed through the air. One smashed behind the vizier, and he jumped. Another crashed at his feet. The last one hit him in the chest.

Hah!

He roared with rage.

I kept going.

So did he. Tearing everything to shreds with his magic. Pillows exploded, pumping stuffing everywhere. Chairs exploded into thousands of pieces. Glass from the lamps rained down over me. The acrid smell of burned fabric drowned my nostrils.

For a few blows, I hid behind his sofa until he turned it into sawdust.

Dark magic sliced through my arm, and I screamed. Instead of blood gushing out, the wound festered with bubbling black goo.

Clutching my arm, I scrambled to my feet.

Dead ahead, the column called for me. It was now or never. I made a run for it.

The vizier aimed all his hatred at me. Buzzing black projections sailed past me. One gazed my leg, and I yelped. Not even my limp stopped me. My legs pumped hard, pushing me the last bit of distance. Just as Zand had calculated, the vizier's final blow cut the pillar right through the middle.

A laugh rumbled in my chest that he'd been stupid enough to fall for our plan.

The column groaned as it teetered. Down it crashed, sending vibrations rattling through my bones. The roof creaked and sagged as it lost one of its supports.

The vizier's piercing shriek sounded as if it belonged to a thousand dead souls.

Tremors rocked the palace. Cracks traveled along the marble floors and walls. The whole place groaned as if about to collapse. A split several meters deep opened up in the ground. The stand storing the dark flame toppled and smashed. It burned into the floor like acid. How it had not done the same to the stand, I did not know.

The magical barriers holding the genies went out with a crackle and snap.

Horror claimed the vizier's face. "I'll kill you for that, you insolent street rat," he screamed.

Hope thawed the iciness inside me.

Flames zipped across Zand and Dahvi until the fire covered every inch of their skin. Vengeance didn't begin to describe the gleam in their eyes. They were going to kill the vizier before he hurt me.

Zand limped forward, spinning a fiery lasso. Dahvi shot out watery darts that hit the vizier. His body sizzled, and he screamed. A lasso whooshed through the air, hooking the vizier. Zand gave a yank, and the vizier crashed to his knees. The vizier roared, and black balls ejected from him. Both genies blocked them with fiery shields. But each strike ate away at their magic. Zand didn't have much left and teetered on the edge of mortality.

I ran to Ali's side out on the balcony and shielded him. Blood trickled down his forehead. Each time my gaze darted to one of his bruises, a tornado whisked through my blood.

"Azar," he said, lifting a weak finger behind me.

Something exploded behind us. Chunks of the wall smashed on the floor some feet away from us. I crushed my brother's head to me. Those blocks scraped across the ground, coming right for us.

Fear shackled me to the floor as marble trapped us.

"Zand, Dahvi," I screamed.

The vizier stomped toward me. Clasped in his hands was a long black sword, dripping with black goo. Made from dark flame. Designed to kill me and probably destroy my soul at the same time.

Behind him, Zand and Dahvi were on the floor, clambering to their feet. The vizier must have bowled them over with a powerful attack.

Terror chased through me as the marble chunks squeezed my brother and me. I clutched him for dear life. My brother shrieked in my ear. Sobs racked my throat. I'd failed him. Let him down. What a disappointment of a sister. Found three genies and still couldn't save him. Talk about an absolute loser.

Hatred burned in the vizier's eyes as he raised the sword above his head.

Ice stabbed my guts.

A flash of red burst behind him.

The vizier jolted as a burning blue spear pierced his chest. He gasped and fell to his knees. Choking noises came out of his mouth. His hands weakly gripped the spear, trying to pull it out.

The pressure from the marble chunks eased on my brother and me.

"Sorcerer," growled Zand, hobbling over to the vizier. The dark flame flickered in his palm, staining it black. "Today, you threatened my family. Now I claim the right of the djinn to destroy your inner flame."

I didn't quite understand that because only genies and djinn had inner flames. Did that mean Zand was going to strip the vizier of his evil power? Whatever it meant, I was totally fine with it. But I still flinched as Zand thrust the dark flame into the vizier's chest. The magic spread across the evil sorcerer, eating away at him until there was nothing left but ash. Zand's chest heaved as he stood over the remains of the vizier.

Relief teamed in my veins as Dahvi shifted the barricade around Ali and me.

My heroes. My protectors.

I was shaking like a palm tree when Dahvi wrapped his arms around Ali and me.

"Thank you," I cried into his chest.

The genie brushed my hair from my face and kissed the top of my head. I wanted to stay in his arms forever.

Behind him, Zand used his magic to burn the chains from Ali's wrists.

My brother made a brave face, even though I could tell the heat stung him. The chains dropped to the ground.

"Thanks, Zand," Ali said, rubbing his swollen and bruised wrists.

The genie ruffled his hair. "Anything for my brother."

I basked in the warmth that flowed between them.

I ran my hands all over Ali's face, neck, shoulders, and chest, searching for injuries. "Ali, are you hurt?"

He rubbed his wrists. "Just a little bruised and broken. But if Ali Baba can handle it," he said referring to his favorite comic book hero, "then I can, too."

A relieved laugh rumbled in my chest.

He pushed me away and clasped my hands. "Azar, stop fussing. I'm okay."

Part of me knew he was putting on a brave face for the genies. The way he puffed out his chest, acting macho, told me so. How could he not with all his new brothers surrounding him? A deeper, more sacred part of me understood my baby brother was becoming a man. His newfound attitude had blossomed in the genies' company. Call it the big brother affect.

My heart sagged in my chest. Ali was his own man now. But I worried that he'd get too attached to the genies. Zand had called me his mate, but in less than a month, he'd belong to The Collector. Dahvi had promised me he was mine forever. But who knew what Kaza's plans were once our business was concluded. I didn't want to break Ali's heart.

MILA YOUNG

There was still the news of Karim to report. One heartbreak was enough for my brother.

Ali gave Zand a teasing tap on the shoulder. "You know I could have escaped those chains Ali Baba style?"

Zand raised a sarcastic eyebrow. "Want to demonstrate?"

Ali leaped onto the genie, engaging in a light-hearted wrestle. My stomach tightened at the idea of my brother getting hurt. Obviously Ali wasn't thinking about his health. The laughter sprouting from them both spoke of their enjoyment.

Clearly, they'd been having a bit too much fun while I'd been away from home on errands. For now, I'd let them enjoy each other's company and discuss it later. Luckily, their horseplay didn't last long, interrupted when a coughing fit doubled Ali over. Zand cleared that up with a thump on my brother's back.

While Zand and my brother kept each other busy, I had another job to do. Free Kaza. From across the room, I spied a hint of his normal color returning to his skin, and my chest lit awake. But as I crossed the room, someone blocked my path.

The djinn, her expression hard and cold, promising me retribution for kicking her in the face, stood before me.

CHAPTER 16

Shock wedged my breath somewhere between my toes and head. *Crap.* What did she want? To return the punch I'd given her in the nose? Kill me because she didn't approve of me as a mate for her kin?

Whatever the answer, I kept a wary distance from her.

Black tendrils covering her body turned to dust and blew away. The bindings on her wrists dropped to the ground and melted on the marble. Now she was free of the vizier's spell holding her captive in the city.

She reached out to touch me, and I recoiled.

"Sorry about your nose," I said, hoping this was enough for her to leave me alone.

Her fingers traced the crusty blood on the edge of her nostrils. "You have the heart of a djinn. A fire within you. I understand why my brothers consider you their mate."

Heart of a djinn? What the hell did that mean? I didn't possess an inner flame or any magic. She must have hit her head a lot harder than I'd thought. I wrapped my arms around my waist as she retreated.

"Great, thanks for freeing me, Brothers," she told Zand and Dahvi.

Zand climbed off Ali to press his forehead to hers.

"Can you forgive me?" she asked, clasping the back of his neck.

Zand clapped a meaty hand on her back. "Of course, Sister. But you owe us a debt under djinn law."

Behind them, Ali looked at me and mouthed the words, *who's that?*

I shrugged, planning on telling him later. Right now, I wanted to make sure she kept her mitts of my man. My hands fisted in case she tried anything funny, ready to send her down for the count for a second time today.

She smiled and bowed. "Ask of me what you will."

"I owe a debt to a woman named Red who dwells in the land of the Darkwoods." His jaw tightened as he glanced at me. "Serve in my place, and void my agreement with her."

Excitement washed across my heart. Was that even possible? It bloody well better be. I didn't want to lose Zand or any of my genies, especially not to that freaky weirdo, The Collector. I held my breath, waiting for the djinn to agree to the deal.

Her posture turned rigid as if she didn't like the idea of service after just being freed. "Three wishes? That is all?"

Zand nodded. "And I also promised her my brother's flying carpet."

Her jaw tightened. "Very well. Bring me the carpet."

I blinked, not believing she'd consented so easily. No one in Haven would have agreed to that crappy deal after they were freed from imprisonment. But I didn't say a thing, not wanting her to change her mind.

Dahvi said something in a foreign language and his carpet sailed through the vizier's window.

"Come," the Shaitan told the carpet.

Sand whirled around the djinn and carried her away, out the window and into the sky.

Thank the gods. I didn't want her around any longer than necessary. The words "psycho bitch" came to mind.

"I can't believe she agreed," I said, throwing my arms around Zand's neck.

"It is djinn law," said Zand, placing a sweet kiss on my lips. "If she refuses, the spirits of the dead djinn will haunt her until her dying day."

That didn't sound very comforting. I certainly wouldn't want to be hounded by ghosts intent on pressuring me into delivering a favor.

I stared into Zand's eyes. All brown now, without the red rim, as using his magic had depleted him. After the effort he'd just expended to save us, I wasn't surprised. He'd need a good week of rest. Preferably in bed beside me. Don't know how we would fit all three genies in my tiny shack. The bed was only big enough for Ali and me. But we'd figure it out. I probably wasn't going to be getting much sleep, anyway, sneaking off with my new mates.

"Gross," said Ali at mine and Zand's smooch. "Get a room!"

Zand and I laughed.

Dahvi came up behind us, carrying Kaza.

"Thanks for the sands, Brother." Kaza gave Zand a hug.

What? Dahvi had given Kaza the sands of Katar already? I glanced down at the yellow genie's leg and it had healed. Amazing. I clasped my hands together. I waited patiently for my turn to hug my fun loving genie.

Zand smirked and patted Kaza's shoulder. "Enjoy the fart, Brother?"

Kaza punched Zand's arm. "You're in for a world of pain."

Zand rubbed Kaza's hair. "I welcome it."

I couldn't help it. A snort came out. After all my trouble

of late, I looked forward to some good laughs. Just not the camel poo in my pillow kind. Gods. What was Kaza going to do to my shack in his quest for vengeance against Zand?

"Isn't our desert queen sexy, Brother?" Kaza asked Zand.

The red genie grunted his approval.

This time, I pinched Kaza on the behind. "Desert queen's better than Master."

He chuckled and slapped my ass.

"Guys, you're making me ill," joked Ali in between little coughs.

Zand whacked him on the shoulder, bringing on a severe splutter. What should have been over and done with a few coughs turned into a longer-than-usual episode. The last time this happened, my brother couldn't breathe. The genie tapped Ali's back to calm him down, but that just made things worse, and he gasped for air.

My heart hammered against my ribcage. "Ali, I'll get you some water."

I hurried away to the sounds of his croaks. When I returned with a pitcher from the vizier's side table, Ali's eyes bulged, and he gasped for air. Zand's thumps on Ali's chest stopped his hacks, and he wheezed for breath.

My brother didn't have a week. All the excitement and danger was making him sicker.

I lifted the pitcher to his lips, and he took a sip.

"Azar," he said, clutching my so tight I lost circulation to my hands. "It's getting worse. I...I need the medicine. Now."

My insides crumbled, and words tangled on my tongue. I didn't know what to do. My genie's hearts revealed they were dark with sorrow for not having enough power to create gold coins to help Ali. I glanced at each of them, seeking guidance.

Dahvi lifted the flame-shaped decoration from around his necklace. "We could sell this to raise the funds."

"No, Brother." Zand touched Dahvi's chest. "It's all you have left of your family."

I agreed. The genie was not sacrificing the last reminder of his heritage. We'd find another way. I always did. If it required me to steal something else, then I'd do it.

Dahvi pulled away. "Why do you always get to be the hero?"

Zand ducked his head as if his brother's words stung.

Fighting amongst ourselves was not going to solve anything. I advanced across the room, looking for something that had belonged to the vizier—something we might sell. Anything that wasn't smashed from our battle. I found a lamp stand with thick, heavy gold legs, and an inlaid gold-legged recliner, but both were too heavy to carry down to the pawnshop.

"We need something light to trade," I announced. "Jewels work best."

Kaza lifted his head to look at me. "The vizier has two golden skulls I saw him use in a ritual."

The idea of the vizier worshipping some dark god made me quiver. After what the dark flame had done to me, I didn't want to touch anything used for dark magic.

"No," I said. "Nothing magical."

Zand stepped forward. "Dark magic needs to be eliminated."

Dahvi nodded. "Wrap the skulls in cloth. Have them smelted to eliminate its power."

That idea filled me with a buzz. I'd do anything to prevent someone else from getting hurt by creeps like the vizier. Once the sultan found out about the vizier's death, the sultan would most likely put the skulls in his cave with all his other treasures. That left them open for someone else to steal. Someone who knew dark magic. No. No way.

"It's settled then," I said with a smile.

"Hurry back, my desert queen," warned Zand, limping as he carried my brother toward the staircase.

I took off, in search of the mysterious skulls. In the next chamber, I located them sitting on an altar covered in burning incense and candles. I wrapped them, along with a few rings and broaches, in silks and carried them back to Dahvi and Kaza who waited for me at the top of the stairs.

By the time we emerged out of the tunnel, the afternoon sun sat directly overhead, glaring down on us. Even with his darkened skin tone, my brother looked pale.

"Wait for me by the river," I said to the genies and Ali.

Zand limped forward in protest. "You can't go alone."

I had to. Zand, Kaza, and Ali were weak. They needed Dahvi to watch over them. Me, on the other hand, I was used to going things alone. With the vizier gone, I wasn't worried about the consequences. I kissed Zand's hand, my brother's forehead, and gave the other two genies a quick smooch on the lips.

"If I'm not back in two rotations of the sand glass," I said. "Come looking for me."

* * *

SOMETIME LATER, I arrived at the smelter on the outer limits of the city.

Before I entered, I removed the rings and broaches and slipped them into my pocket. Thick smoke piped out the furnace on the roof. The place stank like fire and molten metal.

"Hello," I called out, admiring the metalworking tools and a raging furnace inside the workshop. The heat was intense, bringing on an instant sheen of sweat all over my body.

A middle-aged man with a stiff hip appeared a few moments later, carrying a freshly forged sword like those used by the palace guards. He dipped the glowing orange metal in a well of water, and it hissed and cooled. His skin was covered in grime and glistened with sweat.

"What can I do for you?" the metal smelter asked.

I pulled the skulls out from the silks. "I'd like to smelt these in exchange for one thousand markos."

The blacksmith's eyes widened, and he reached out a hand. "Where'd you get those?"

"Do you want them or not?" I folded one edge of the silk over the skulls.

"Don't be hasty," said the trader. "I'll give you five hundred markos for them."

Five hundred? What a joke! Did he think me a fool? A thief like me knew the value of gold and other such treasures. I wrapped the goods and turned to leave.

"Eight hundred," the trader stuttered.

I considered the offer for a few moments. The broach and ring should cover the additional two hundred markos I needed for Ali's medicine. But I had extra mouths to feed now. The genies, my brother, and I also needed some food and water.

I turned to face the trader. "Nine hundred and you have a deal."

He wiped his forehead with the back of his hand. "Give me a moment." He shuffled away and returned a few seconds later carrying a velvet pouch.

We exchanged the items. I loosened the strings on the bag and tipped it upside down, spilling the coins in my palm. I counted them. Nine one-hundred markos. Perfect.

"Thank you," I said, returning the coins to the pouch.

The smelter was transfixed with the gold skulls. "Pleasure doing business with you." The way he said this raised my suspicions, but I didn't stop to contemplate his meaning because I had to get to the pawnshop, then the apothecary for Ali's medicine.

I ran as fast as I could through the city, pushing my ankle and lungs to their limits to get to the pawnshop.

Once I had another five hundred markos in my pocket, I pushed onto to the medicine shop. Along the way, I got stuck in a large crowd, and had to shove my way through. When I finally arrived, the awnings were pulled down over the windows, and my heart sank to the bottom of my chest.

Damn. The store had closed.

But when a customer dressed in a cotton thobe emerged, I bustled past him and through the doorway. The bell tinkled as the door slammed closed after me. Inside, the shop smelled of the finest-quality incense and herbs. A new stand had been erected since I'd last visited, which held shelves of teapots and packets of various leaf brews.

I emptied the velvet pouch of markos onto the counter. "I want to buy dragon's thistle oil."

The shop owner blinked several times and dropped the giant sack of herbs he carried. "Where did you get this?" He bit one of the coins as if he thought them fake.

I stared at him hard. "Does it matter?"

The shop owner brushed the coins off the counter into his waiting palm. "I will need a week to prepare it."

"No." I gripped the counter. "I need it now. Do you have any? I'll take an old batch. My brother's health is declining."

"Wait here." The owner disappeared into the back of the shop.

I paced along the sandstone floor, praying to the gods with every fiber of my being that there was some oil left. I'd come too far to fail. They couldn't let me down now. Not when my world teetered on a knife's edge.

Some moments later, the shop owner returned carrying a small vial full of a honey-colored liquid. "This is only two doses worth. Your brother will need five in total. One every three days. This should tide him over until I can make the rest."

I raced behind the counter and gave the man a hug. "Oh, thank you. Thank you." I kissed him on the hand.

The shop owner patted me on the back of my wrist. "Come back in five days. I will have the rest ready for you."

EPILOGUE

our rotations of the moon had passed, and things had finally settled down after the vizier's death. The dragon's thistle medicine had cured Ali's dark lung. It had taken a few weeks for the genies' power to restore to full capacity. Then they had worked their magic to create all my wishes and more. Back in Utaara, the sultan had called in all the builders in Utaara to rebuild the slums. New townhouses and apartment blocks rose from the ashes left behind by the dead creep. My heart warmed, knowing all of my neighbors would receive fresh accommodations.

I glanced around my own new home. A five-bedroom mansion by the sea with salmon-colored walls, wooden floors, high ceilings, and plenty of windows to welcome the coastal breeze. The air was thick with the scent of baked Barbari bread thanks to Dahvi's skills in the kitchen.

Zand delivered breakfast to the table out on the deck overlooking the coast—an assortment of tapas laid out on the dish, cucumbers, feta cheese, olives, jam, and other condiments.

"I'll never get used to being spoiled," I told him, giving his butt a little love tap.

"Nor should you, my desert queen." He laid a big one on my lips.

I grabbed his wrist where he used to wear the gold bands holding him captive to the genie lamp. Gods, I was so glad my men had stayed with me once I had released them from their service.

I added five plates and only two sets of utensils to the table. The genies ate with their fingers; it was their culture, so I left them to it as a little reminder of home.

Teacups rattled as Dahvi set them on the dinner table. Zand added the pot to a woven mat in the center of the counter. I smiled in thanks as he poured me a cup of a cinnamon-scented brew.

Ali and Kaza had the morning off breakfast duties and sat waiting for their meal.

I gave the tops of their heads a kiss before I took my seat at my usual place on the opposite side of the table away from the fireplace. It wasn't like we needed the extra heat. Our home by the coast was warm and tropical. But my genies thrived on the fire. They claimed it stoke their inner flame and connected them to their magic. Well...what little remained after they'd sacrificed it for a life with me.

"Oh, come on," said Kaza, with a playful punch on Ali's upper arm. "Are you telling me there's no special girl in your life?"

"Gods," said Ali, covering his eyes. "Can you put a shirt on? I'm sick of looking at your nipples."

I snorted, hot tea spewing from my lips.

Once I had freed them, they had thrown out their vests. They'd also taken to walking around without anything covering their chests. Didn't bother me. I got to perv all day long. But my poor brother didn't feel the same way. I didn't blame him. He was young and reedy, waiting to fill out, and having three gorgeous, ripped genies living in the same house probably gave him an inferiority complex.

A hearty laugh rolled in Kaza's throat as a shirt with the words *I Love Genies* on the front suddenly appeared on him. Dahvi and Zand shared a smile, plucking their own shirts out of thin air—a singlet for Zand, which showed off every muscle in his chest and arms. Gods, he may as well have been wearing nothing. Not that I was complaining. Dahvi wore a shirt similar to Kaza's that read, *Genies Rock*.

That was it. I was done. I slumped over the table giggling. These four made me laugh so much. This was how things usually were during our mealtimes. At least it wasn't boring. I'd found my soul mates, Ali had three big brothers who'd protect him just as I had, and the genies scored an even bigger family.

Zand sat down beside me and patted his thigh. That was my cue to sit on his lap. I did so, positioning myself sideways, and he wrapped an arm around my waist. I rested my legs on Dahvi, and he massaged my foot.

Gods, I enjoyed being spoiled.

Kaza stuffed a cheese-and-jam bread slice into his mouth. "Spit it out, little brother. Who's the girl? I know there is one. I'm the love god."

Everyone at the table got stitches from that one. Although, Kaza had given me his heart and had claimed me as his only mate, he was still a ladies' man. Always charming our housekeeper, Ali's schoolteachers, stallholders in the market... But the flirty flattery was as far as it went. That's the way I liked it.

Gods. I rubbed a hand to my forehead. The last thing I wanted to hear about was Kaza's past escapades with other women.

Kaza winked, prompting Ali to spill the beans.

Red pinched my poor brother's cheeks. "Well. There is one."

"Does she have big breasts and a small waist?" asked Zand as he munched on some bread dipped in oil.

I cleared my throat.

"Don't worry." Zand ripped off a piece of lamb and patted my thighs. "She'd never compare to my desert queen."

Damn, I loved it when he called me that.

"Why don't you go talk to her?" encouraged Kaza.

Ali ducked his head. "She'd never look at me."

My brother had never spoken to any girls. The poor kid was too shy.

Kaza washed his breakfast down with tea. "She will once you use some complimentary lines to woo her."

Ali stuffed an olive in his mouth, going even redder.

Kaza loved teasing him. I think it made him feel like he had a younger brother. I guessed now that we were all family, that was the case.

Zand rubbed my thigh with his free hand, and I squeezed it back.

Dahvi tickled my foot, and I flinched, poking my tongue out at him.

"You'll like this one, my desert queen." Kaza blew me a kiss from across the table. Then he turned back to Ali. "Was your father a thief? Because someone stole the stars from the sky and put them in your eyes."

I moaned. "Does that actually work?"

Dahvi went to answer, but I raised my hand, stopping him.

"Never mind," I said, "I don't want to know."

"Oh, oh." Kaza bounced in his chair. "I've got a good one."

Even Ali seemed amused for a change.

"Are you a genie?" Kaza made everyone wait in suspense

for a few moments before delivering the end. "Because whenever I look at you, everyone else disappears!"

We all laughed.

"I'm not saying that." Ali shook his head and chewed some cheese, jam, and bread.

Kaza dunked a cucumber slice in some dip. "Trust me. She'll love it."

I wasn't so sure of that. If Ali's love interest was half as smart as I was, she'd see through any corny lines. Besides, that wasn't really Ali's style.

Kaza patted Ali's chest with the back of his hand. "Do you have a map? I'm getting lost in your eyes."

Zand got a chuckle from that one.

Kaza kept pestering Ali throughout the remainder of breakfast.

This sort of banter was pretty much how every meal went. And that's how I liked it.

Once Zand and Dahvi were finished, they were out the door. Zand, to collect wood for the fireplace he kept ablaze all day long. Dahvi, to do his morning yoga. That was cool with me. I'd gotten into the habit of watching them. Something I'd never tire of.

So far I was pretty content with the way my life had turned around. I had my own home by the ocean, a larger-than-life family, and enough money to never worry about anything again.

The genies still possessed a little magic, but far from the great expanses they used to harness. It was enough to whip up a meal here and there, give me a rose, and take the magic carpet for a spin. But doing so made them tired and in need of a rest.

I spent part of my days preparing plans to build my orphanage and school. At mealtimes I would join Dahvi in the kitchen. My nights were consumed with pleasure and passion with my men. I'd never been happier. Every day I couldn't keep the smile from my face. I was so grateful to the gods. For once in my life my future looked incredibly bright. I was very excited for what else lay in store for my family and me.

But for now I had a big secret I was about to unveil to Ali. I couldn't wait to show him. I tiptoed down the corridor to the little cage in my room.

"Hello there," I said, opening the cage door to give the little furry thing with the big expressive eyes inside it a scratch on its chin.

It squeaked at me and nibbled on my finger.

I laughed, picking it up. "Oh no. I'm not a banana." The little squeaker cuddled my neck, and I stroked its soft back. "My brother's going to love you."

I carried the monkey out into the living room where my brother was reading one of his books and Kaza was smoking a hookah pipe.

"Ali," I said. "I've got someone I want you to meet."

"It's not a girl is it?" He sunk into his sofa, and hid behind his book.

Kaza snatched it away. "Damn right it's a girl."

"No, Azar. Please don't embarrass me and introduce me to another girl." When Ali glanced up at me his face blanched and his lips wobbled. "Is that for me?"

My throat choked up, and I nodded. News of Karim's death had crushed my brother. He'd grieved for over a rotation of the moon. I'd given him time to process his monkey's death. Then I'd ordered another squeaker from a merchant in town. It only arrived by messenger this morning.

"Her name's Karima," joked Kaza, slapping Ali with the back of his hand.

Ali laughed. "That's a stupid name."

I handed Ali the monkey.

He clutched it to his chest as if it were his own baby. "Hello. You're very cute. And you don't smell as bad as Karim."

Tears streamed down his cheeks.

Damn it. He made me cry too.

"And you're a girl too," said Ali. "What shall I call you?"

"Kazana," suggested Kaza.

"No way," Ali replied.

Zand entered with a stack of logs in his arms.

"Zandi," Kaza said.

"No."

"Careful," Zand said, throwing a log onto the fire.

"Dahvina," tried Kaza.

"Gods." Ali slapped a hand over his forehead.

Kaza crossed his arms. "What about Ali Baba?"

Ali's frown softened. He thought about it for a few moments. "It's a boy's name. But I like it."

That was settled then.

Ali jumped and gave me a quick hug. "Thank you, Azar."

I rubbed his back. "You're welcome."

Things were finally coming together. Everything was perfect. I'd gotten my happy ending, and I couldn't ask for it any other way.

Thanks for reading Charmed.

Reviews are super important to authors as it helps other reader make better decisions on books they will read. So if you have a moment, please do leave a review for Hunted, HERE.

Are you curious to read the next Haven Realm instalment about Bee and her adventures into the White Peak Mountains where the deadly bear shifters live? Discover more in **CURSED.**

Beauty and the Four Beasts. A Deadly Curse. A Fallen Kingdom.

With magic banned in the human realm, Bee, a powerful witch, has had to offer her services in secret. When a request to break a curse comes from the dangerous mountains and royal bear shifters, Bee is hesitant, but winter is coming and funds are tight.

At the castle, Bee finds things are not quite what she was led to believe. The curse Bee is meant to break has reached its zenith, siphoning off the Prince's life while preventing him from controlling his shifting abilities. He is volatile, angry, and far stronger than she had imagined. His brothers, who commissioned her, present her with a challenge - fix it, or lose everything.

Soon the curse is spreading throughout the castle, taking brother and servant alike. It's a race against the clock, buffeted by dark magic, intrigue, and a strange attraction that has her looking at the four brothers in a new light.

Click To Read Bee's Tale in Cursed

* * *

Subscribe to Mila Young's Newsletter to receive exclusive content, latest updates, and giveaways. Join here.

HAVEN REALM SERIES
Hunted
Charmed
Cursed

Continue the Haven Realm series.
www.amazon.com/Mila-Young/e/B077QT5J5M

HUNTED

Little Red Riding Hood. Three Big Bad Wolves. A Poisonous Scheme.

Scarlet, a healer, lives nestled in the forest surrounded by humans on one side and wolves on the other. But when a rogue wolf attacks her, she's rescued by another pack and taken deep into their den to perform her healing magic on an injured Alpha.
The wolves in the forest are under threat from a mysterious affliction, and Scarlet is the only hope they have left. Faced with a mixed pack of threatened shifters, Scarlet must use her wits and magic to survive and unravel the strange affliction now affecting the wolves... All while trying to navigate an overpowering attraction to not just one, but three of the Alphas.
Witches, wolves, magic and love intertwine in an exciting mystery that finds its own, unique, 'Happily Ever After.'

Click To Read Hunted

HAVEN REALM SERIES
Hunted
Charmed
Cursed

Continue the Haven Realm series.

www.amazon.com/Mila-Young/e/B077QT5J5M

HUNTED EXCERPT

 **hapter 1**

"SCARLET, GET A LOOK AT HIM." Bee nudged me in the ribs.

I gritted my teeth, my hands juggling the jar of chamomile I'd just pulled off the shelf. "For the love of wolfsbane."

Honestly, Bee had the boniest elbow in all the seven realms of Haven. No matter how often I protested, she insisted on jabbing me right in the side every time she had something to say. Her idea of grabbing my attention wasn't tapping my shoulder but inflicting pain. I twisted around and my gaze flew through the arched windows of my store, Get Your Herb On.

A huge guy marched out of the woods, arms swinging in an over-exaggerated motion. His chest stuck out, and with his chin high, I had him figured out in two seconds flat. I'd seen so many of his kind leaving the priestess's palace.

Guardians, full of cockiness and attitude, taking what they wanted without paying for goods.

Yet he wasn't wearing a uniform, but the strangest clothes. A gray tunic falling to mid-thigh; no pants or boots. Goddess, his legs were the size of tree trunks.

"Who wants to bet his muscles aren't real?" I said. I'd heard of people using magic to enhance their physique. It was the latest trend in other territories.

Bee glanced at me with disbelief pinching her expression. With her braided red hair and ivory skin, most called her beautiful and always referenced her green eyes. But the real Bee was also tough. I'd once seen her scare off a bear with a glare, and there was a reason most in town kept their distance from her. Sure, it might have a little something to do with Bee insisting most of the folk were uneducated swine breeders—her words, not mine—but hey, she was a best friend who often popped into my store, and I loved her company. Even if she didn't know when to keep her mouth shut.

"How can they not be real?" Her gaze turned from the man and back my way. "He's not wearing pants. What could he possibly be padding—" Then her eyes widened, and her lips curled upward into a wicked grin. "You filthy girl, Scarlet. Never knew you had it in you." She whacked me in the arm, her strength intimidating, considering she stood five-foot-two and reached my nose.

"What are you talking about?" I slouched, a hip pressed against the counter, and pushed several sample bowls of tea leaves up against the ceramic cups that I had painted with different stages of the moon cycle. I called them my night collection series and regular customers tended to buy a new one whenever they purchased their regular healing herbs. If I had more time, I'd paint all the time.

"You're referring to his junk, aren't you? And well…" Bee

glanced outside. "With the wind blowing against his clothes, there's definitely a healthy package in his arsenal." Bee wiggled her eyebrows and broke out laughing.

Fire scorched my cheeks. You'd think I'd be used to Bee's dirty mouth; after all, this was normal for her. "I wasn't talking about his… his privates."

Bee gripped her hips, cinching in the long, blue tunica dress she wore. The outfit had a V-neckline and tiny buttons ran down the front. I admired her flowing sleeves, and I needed to re-examine my wardrobe. My black pants and sea-green blouse beneath the leather vest with a belt made me look more like a thief. But when I chose my clothing, I prioritized comfort. Most days, I lifted boxes at work and a skirt would get in the way.

"Just say it, Scarlet," Bee continued. "Dick. Cock."

I rolled my eyes. I had no issues with such words… As long as I didn't say them. I blamed my grandma, who'd brought me up strict, no cursing or vulgarities. Heavens bless her soul.

"Penis." Bee licked her lips. "Blowjob."

A squeaky male's voice came from behind Bee. "Eww." Santos walked out of the storage room carrying several boxes. "I can hear you out the back. That's called sexual harassment of men."

I sighed, loathing that Santos had heard our conversation, and Bee spun toward my eighteen-year-old apprentice. But he might as well be fourteen with his thin frame, shaved hair, and his maturity level. Then again, were Bee and myself any better?

"Hey, guys talk crap about girls all the time," Bee said. "What's the difference?"

Santos set the three boxes of tobacco leaves on the end of the counter. "You two are too old to talk about such things, and it's gross."

"Old?" Bee's voice climbed. "We're only a year older than you." She turned to me with a cocked eyebrow, expecting me to say something. I shrugged my shoulders.

"That's okay, Santos," I said. "We'll curb our tongues if it makes you uncomfortable." He worked his butt off, and I didn't need him leaving. He'd been working for me for a year and had just learned the names of all the dried plants we sold.

"It's fine." He didn't glance our way and instead opened the first box and scooped handfuls of tobacco into tiny satchels.

I marched to the opposite end of the counter. Bee followed me, probably ready to offer one of her smartass comments about Santos, but I jumped in first to change the direction of the conversation. "How come you're not wearing your new boots? The ones I got you for Christmas?"

Bee huffed. "Can't get them dirty, as I plan to wear them to the town ball. Might attract myself a prince in disguise. Besides, you live in the woods with lots of mud and—"

The front doorbell chimed, stealing her words.

We all glanced up to find Mr. No Pants bursting into the shop with a flurry, his breaths labored and his cheeks red.

"I need help," he wheezed.

"My, what do we have here?" Bee said, drawing the newcomer's attention to the three sets of eyes on him… mine lowering to his legs, and even with his tunic covering, he had a huge package. But I focused on the red bleeding through his tunic at his hip. How had he gotten injured? Animal attack?

At once, Mr. No Pants straightened his posture and flicked his raven hair over a shoulder, his sights sliding from me to Bee, then locking on to her curvy chest.

Okay, he was a womanizer. Score another point for Bee against Santos in the women versus men chauvinist race.

The newcomer could at least have had the decency to keep his eyes above neck level.

Bee pulled the elastic free from her braid and fluffed out her hair. Typical. I nudged her and raised my eyebrows.

"Geez, live a little, Scarlet," she whispered. "You've been too sheltered."

I tucked a lock behind an ear. "Brown as a deer," my grandma had once called my hair. Nothing sexy about that. Maybe the reason I never got a guy's attention was I stayed too safe.

My sights fell on the newcomer's blood. Was it a human who had shot him with a bow and arrow? I rounded the counter. "Are you all right?"

He stood at least six foot with a solid square jawline, studying me as if I might be an animal he'd crossed paths with in the woods.

"You're injured," I continued.

The man didn't say a word but scanned the room, and then looked out through the windows behind him. "I'm wonderful." Yet he stood there, a trickle of blood rolling down the side of his leg from under his tunic.

"Don't think so," Bee blurted out. "Unless you're a mutant who bleeds instead of sweating, you're about to dirty up Scarlet's floor."

He stared at me, and a brush of desperation shifted behind his eyes. The kind I'd seen when I'd first met Santos over a year ago, when he'd been sleeping on the streets, thin and pasty. Sometimes asking for help was the hardest thing to do.

"Come," I said. "We have a room out back, and I'll bring you hot tea to calm your nerves." I surveyed the dirt road outside and the woods in the distance for anything suspicious. My shop was located in the forest on the fringe of civilization, so I often saw strange things. But it was all clear.

A few weeks ago, in the middle of the night, another buff guy with no shirt had turned up on my doorstep asking for specific plants for healing someone gravely ill. Before that, another man had been at my door, his clothes torn and his butt exposed.

A loser in the town of Terra had scored Get Your Herb On with a one-star on the town review board. The priestess ruling over the Terra realm in Haven had introduced a new system. The Customer Approval Plank, she'd called it, insisting it would assist people in choosing the best shops for their needs.

So now, not only did the scoreboard sit in the main town square for everyone to view, but some troll kept marking my store with one star. Was that person spying on me and noticing naked men at my door? No wonder my business has slowed lately.

Mr. No Pants scoffed and folded his arms across his strong chest, then cringed and lowered them.

"So, you going to buy something or—"

I cut Bee a glare, cutting off her words, then turned to the stranger. And I recognized the desperate need for someone to reach out and make that connection, offer a lending hand. When my grandma had passed away of old age, I'd lost everything. She had been my rock, my family, and without Grandma's support, her tonic soups, her hugs, I hadn't been sure how to go on. She'd raised me after my parents had been torn apart by a pack of wolves. Bee had reached out to me, guiding me to find purpose in life again, so now I'd do the same with this man.

"Come with me," I said and headed to the back, his footsteps trailing behind me. "Santos, can you show him a seat? I'll bring him some tea." Something to ease any pain he felt along with his nerves. Might even encourage him to open up about how he'd gotten hurt.

Without a complaint, the two vanished into the storage room. Bee shook her head, giving me a glare.

"Don't say it," I said.

I rushed to the pot with boiling water Santos had set up for samples. I collected a jar of valerian and arrowroot from the cupboard lining the wall behind me. Teapots, candles, and more tea containers filled the shelves. Together with a pinch of chamomile, the aromatic scent had my shoulders lowering.

Bee was in my ear, and I tensed again. "What if he's a guardian? Do you want to bring the priestess's attention to your business? You know she abhors magic. That's why I do my enchantment spells in the basement at home so no one ever catches me."

"This is just an ordinary tea store," I whispered, lowering my palm over the tea bag.

Bee snatched my wrist and lifted my hand, sparks of white energy dancing across my fingertips. "Right, so this is perfectly normal?"

I'd always had the ability to enhance plants, and my grandma had taught me how to harness the power she'd insisted I shared with nature.

"It's nothing." I lied, well aware that the priestess who ruled over the human district forbade anything non-human related. And punishment came in the form of imprisonment for life. Each of the seven territories in Haven were homes to various races, from wolf shifters in our neighboring land, to mermaids, and rumor spoke of a girl with magical hair. Yep, one day I'd explore Haven, but until then, I'd remain in Terra with other humans, pretending we were pure and everyone else was the freak... according to the ruling priestess. And leaving Terra or strangers entering was prohibited. Hence guardians captured any shifters or intruders in Terra for interrogation, never to be seen again.

"Don't kid yourself, Scarlet. I've heard the priestess infiltrated places like the bakeries in town, convinced their breads were too good to be true. And that the baker engaged in sorcery."

Her words left me jittery because I wanted to believe what I did benefited those in need. I drew on my ability to amplify the strength of herbs, so when people used them, they got the full effect. If chamomile calmed someone, then it put them into such a relaxed state, their anxiety slipped away. What was wrong with that?

"We'll be cautious, then," I suggested.

Bee nodded. "Smart idea. I'll be the bad enforcer and you the good."

"What? Wait, no."

Bee had already steamrolled toward the rear. I left the tea behind and rushed after her.

Santos appeared from the room, his attention sailing to the box of dried tobacco leaves.

"We'll be in the back for a moment," I said.

He nodded. "I've got this." He didn't seem worried in the slightest. Then again, he had no reason to believe the guy was anything but someone in danger, and he had zero idea about my powers.

Once I entered the storage room, I found Bee leaning over Mr. No Pants, who sat on a chair, her index finger pressed against his chest. "Where are your trousers? This isn't a peep show kind of store."

"Bee. Give him space to breathe." Without waiting for a response, I collected my medicine box from the shelves and flipped the lid open. "Now, let's examine your wound."

"How did you get hurt, hmm?" Bee towered over him, her hands gripping her waist. Geez, the girl should train as a guardian.

"I'm not here to harm you. You can relax." He lifted the tunic up and bunched it at his side.

My gaze dove to his midsection like a desperate hound dog. Except the guy wore black underwear.

Bee sighed.

He peeled away fabric stuck to the mess underneath, wincing, and I cringed at how much it must have hurt.

Three claw marks tore across his side, blood everywhere.

"Holy shiitake mushrooms," I said. "What did this to you?"

He cut me a strange look with a raised eyebrow as if he'd pull away from my touch if I tried to treat him.

"Crapping balls, Scarlet. This requires a fuck me, not mushrooms," Bee blurted out. "But really, dude." She turned to the stranger. "This is bad. Like you'll die, that kind of bad. If you want my friend to cure you, talk."

Bee was the queen of exaggeration. The guy only had a few scratches and would survive. "Bring me a bowl of boiling water," I asked her because tact wasn't her forte. I grabbed an old towel from the cupboard and cleaned around his wounds. They didn't require stitching.

"Don't listen to her," I said to Mr. No Pants. "What's your name?"

"Better you don't know." He didn't keep my stare, but instead studied the room as if attempting to appear busy. Yep, right there was the warning Bee had mentioned.

"Look," I said. "I'm happy to help you, but are we in danger if we do? Do you work for the priestess?"

He scrunched his nose. "Gods forbid."

Bee returned with a bowl of water she set on the table, and I drenched the stained fabric before continuing to cleanse the injury.

"Where are you from?" I asked. "The mountains? The wolf Den? Oh, maybe you're one of those desert dwellers." The thought had crossed my mind. The human world was comprised of a massive town with several hundred thousand people. Farms dotted the outskirts, but this man wasn't a local. There was an air about him every girl in Terra would have sniffed out by now, especially if he was single. And I would have heard about it at the monthly town gatherings. The ones where the priestess reminded us of our blessing to be pure along with the latest attempts by other factions to infiltrate our territory. In particular, Terra's number one nemesis, the wolves to our east. "Barbarians who attacked anything that moved," she called them.

"I'm not from Terra." He held his head high, as if having nothing to hide, and his admittance didn't surprise me because it wasn't the first time someone had snuck into Terra for help. And humans did the same all the time, leaving behind our land and entering others for various reasons like falling in love with a lion shifter, or at least that had happened to a bookshop owner back in town.

"Are the guardians after you?" I asked.

Bee gave me the *told you* look. But if you followed the rules, Terra was a safe place most of the time.

"No. There was a wolf. In fact, a pack chased me."

"In Terra?" I asked, squeezing the towel into my fist and returning to wiping his wound. I dabbed a mixture of my pre-made antiseptic onto his injuries, and he didn't grimace once.

"Nope. On wolf territory, in the Den. I was passing through and took a shortcut across their land and yours." He paused and wiped his mouth. "But a vicious pack found me and hunted me. I barely escaped with my life before they ripped my pants off."

Bee burst out laughing, her hand pressed over her stomach. "You sure it wasn't a pack of she-wolves?"

He straightened himself. "Girls throw themselves at me

all the time, so I'm guessing the wolves who attacked me instead of ravishing me were males."

Holding back the giggle in my throat, I placed a bandage on his wounds and wrapped it around his waist, then tucked the loose ends in on each other. "There—"

A piercing hoot sounded somewhere outside, and my feet cemented to the ground.

"Fuck," Bee said. "That's the guardians." She shoved a hand into Mr. No Pants' shoulder. "You said they weren't after you."

His face blanched, and he leaped to his feet, towering over us, his top falling over his hips "They aren't. But I have to go."

"Wait, you're still injured, and—"

He placed a hand to my mouth. "Hush."

I pushed his arm away. "Excuse me, who do you think you are?"

"Is there a rear exit?" he asked, his voice low and carrying an air of panic.

Bee stood in the doorway. "Tell us what's going on and we'll let you leave."

The man laughed deep and raw, almost terrifying. "Little girls, you cannot stand in my way. But I will leave you with a warning because you aided me. The wolves are at war amongst themselves. And one fight always spills over in other lands. I was attacked right on the Terra border."

"But we've got wolfsbane dividing our land. That'll keep the packs at bay," I called out as he stormed away from me and lifted Bee out of the doorway as if she were a doll. He then sprinted faster than anyone his size should have been able to.

Santos entered the storeroom. "Where'd he go in such a rush?"

Bee and I exchanged glances as dread threaded through

my chest. I glanced out through the front windows and spotted two guardians in uniform darting left. I sure hoped Mr. No Pants had escaped. It wasn't the first time I'd seen them chase trespassers in Terra, and if I kept my head low, the guardians left me and my store alone. "Well, he wasn't from Terra," I said. "No wonder the guardians are after him."

"He's a looney." Bee wove her arm around mine and guided me back into the main area. "You should consider a lock on the door and only let people in after you study them through the window."

I nodded. She had a point, yet in the back of my mind, I couldn't ignore Mr. No Pants' warning. It wasn't the first time the wolves had attempted to claim territory. They had entered our land before my time, and hundreds of innocent lives had been lost on both sides.

"Do you think the priestess knows about the wolf war?" I asked.

"For sure. Otherwise, what else would her job entail? Oh, right." She cocked a brow. "Controlling all of us. Anyway, I should return home before the sun goes down. Do you have any wolfsbane?"

For those few seconds, Bee's words didn't register as I remained caught up in the whole wolves warring thing and the half-naked stranger at my store, who hadn't even given us his name. Perhaps a lock on the door to protect us from crazy customers wasn't such a bad suggestion.

Bee poked a finger into my arm. "Hello, Scarlet, are you with us?"

Shaking, I hurried to the counter and pushed aside the fabric underneath, concealing the dangerous ingredients. Wolfsbane was poisonous, and I kept it out of view. I plonked the jar on the table, but it was empty and there were a few specs of dust inside. "Well, that's a problem."

Bee gripped her waist. "I thought only I bought the stuff?"

I scratched my head, then remembered where it had gone, but Santos stole my words as he headed into the storage room, calling out his response. "Last week, you added it to the concoction to clean the bird poo off the windows."

"Poo?" Bee paced to the door and back to my side. "But I need it this week. I'm hiking into the mountains to see a client. I assumed you had some." She leaned closer and whispered. "My client claims to have a curse put on him, and I need wolfsbane to create a counter-spell."

Bee practiced magic in secret and was known for her abilities outside of Terra. Here, the priestess would arrest her if she found out, so Bee often sought jobs in other territories for her services.

"Sorry, I'd been meaning to top up the supplies. I'm running out of a few other things too. When did you say you need it by?"

Santos reappeared with the bowl of hot water and bloody towel, heading to the front door to dump the contents outside.

"Tomorrow." Bee twirled a red lock over her shoulder.

"Sweet bolts, that's soon." I hurried to open the front door to hold it for Santos.

"Real sorry, Scarlet. It's just that I received the job this morning."

Santos interrupted. "I can collect some." His eyes were pleading, as he'd wanted to go out on a field excursion forever.

As much as I loved that he offered, I couldn't let him go. "No, it's all right. The plant's dangerous, and I don't want you getting harmed." Plus, I found if I applied my magical touch on plants while still fresh, their intensity worked a treat in spells.

"If it's too hard, I can ask my client if it's all right if we delay the appointment," Bee said, twisting hair around her finger, something she did whenever she was nervous. She and her father struggled financially, and her jobs kept them above the water. I didn't want to cause them any more strain.

"You know I'd do anything for you," I said.

She ran over and drew me into a tight hug, her citrus and vanilla perfume bathing me. "Thanks. And I've always got your back too."

"Sure do!" I giggled, and Bee broke away.

"Okay, I've got to go. Dad's finishing one of his new inventions, and I promised to be his assistant. See you tomorrow? I'll come in the morning?" Bee asked.

"Nah, I'll pop over to your place," I suggested. "You're always saying I spend too much time in the woods instead of society." For the past week, I'd been preparing a paste for her dad, who suffered from joint aches, and planned to finish it tonight to surprise him tomorrow.

Bee hugged me once more and kissed my cheek. She whispered in my ear. "Penis." With a giggle she picked up her satchel from the counter and strolled outside with a wave at Santos before vanishing down the dirt track through the woods.

Santos returned inside. "Yes, I'll watch the place while you're gone. And I promise I won't make any tea pouches and only take orders if anyone needs one."

"You know me too well." I took my coat and bag from the back. Looked like I was making a last-minute trip into the woods. Yet trepidation sat on my shoulders, reminding me of Mr. No Pants' words about the wolves at war. So I grabbed a new bottle of citrus bane mixed with water. The spray would deter any predator coming near me, and when sprayed in anyone's eyes, it made them temporarily blind, giving me time to escape.

ABOUT MILA YOUNG

Mila Young tackles everything with the zeal and bravado of the fairytale heroes she grew up reading about. She slays monsters, real and imaginary, like there's no tomorrow. By day she rocks a keyboard as a marketing extraordinaire. At night she battles with her might pen-sword, creating fairytale retellings, and sexy ever after tales. In her spare time, she loves pretending she's a mighty warrior, walks on the beach with her dogs, cuddling up with her cats, and devouring every fantasy tale she can get her pinkies on.

Ready to read more of Hunted and more from Mila Young? Subscribe today here.

Join Mila's **Wicked Readers group** for exclusive content, latest news, and giveaway. Click here.

For more information...
milayoungauthor@gmail.com

Made in the USA
San Bernardino, CA
09 December 2018